Scent of Death

Emma Page first began writing as a hobby, and after a number of her poems had been accepted by the BBC and her short stories began appearing in weekly magazines, she took to writing radio plays and crime novels. She was first published in the Crime Club, which later became Collins Crime.

An English graduate from Oxford, Emma Page taught in every kind of educational establishment both in the UK and abroad before she started writing full-time.

T0382226

By Emma Page

Kelsey and Lambert series

Say it with Murder
Intent to Kill
Hard Evidence
Murder Comes Calling
In the Event of My Death
Mortal Remains
Deadlock
A Violent End
Final Moments
Scent of Death
Cold Light of Day
Last Walk Home
Every Second Thursday
Missing Woman

Standalone novels

A Fortnight by the Sea (also known as
Add a Pinch of Cyanide)
Element of Chance
In Loving Memory
Family and Friends

Scent of Death

Emma Page

HARPER

This novel is entirely a work of fiction.
The names, characters and incidents portrayed in it are
the work of the author's imagination. Any resemblance to
actual persons, living or dead, events or localities is
entirely coincidental.

Harper
An imprint of HarperCollins*Publishers*
1 London Bridge Street
London SE1 9GF

www.harpercollins.co.uk

This paperback edition 2016
1

First published in Great Britain in 1985 by Collins Crime

Copyright © Emma Page 1985

Emma Page asserts the moral right to
be identified as the author of this work

A catalogue record for this book is
available from the British Library

ISBN: 978-0-00-817584-9

CHAPTER 1

She came blowing into the Railway Tavern in a flurry of
wind and rain on a wild, squally Sunday evening at the end of
February; a short, slight girl, seventeen or eighteen. The
hood of her green anorak was drawn tight round her face, her
black trousers were tucked into wellingtons; she had a
duffel-bag slung across one shoulder. She came to a halt
inside the doorway, gasping and laughing. She undid the
drawstring of her hood and thrust it back, releasing a shower
of raindrops. She ran a hand round the back of her neck and
her long black hair swung out free of the hood. She had a
sharp, resolute face, a pale skin, very dark eyes.

The tavern was a quiet, sober inn; it stood on the outskirts
of Cannonbridge, in a grey, downtrodden area. Not many
folk in this evening, still on the early side. She went up to the
bar and swung the duffel-bag off her shoulder, resting it
against the counter. She loosened the cord and took a large
white envelope from the top of the bag.

A little way along the bar Detective-Sergeant Lambert
stood idly watching as she opened the envelope and drew out
a number of photographs, snapshots mostly, one or two with
the formal, stiff-backed look of studio portraits. She didn't
order a drink, she offered no preamble, she simply held out
the photographs to the barman and asked him, 'Do you know
this girl? She's about the same height and build as me.'

The barman glanced casually at the top snapshot. He
shook his head slowly, in silence.

She jerked the bundle at him impatiently. 'You haven't
looked at them.'

He took the photos from her without enthusiasm and
flicked through them. He shook his head again.

'It could have been a year or two back,' the girl persisted.

'Even three or four years. She might have a different hairstyle from the photographs.'

He shook his head again, with finality. 'No use asking me. I haven't been here twelve months.' He handed her the photographs and she took them reluctantly. He moved away to serve a customer.

She turned her head and glanced along the counter at Lambert. She picked up her duffel-bag and moved towards him. Before she had a chance to speak he said, 'This isn't my usual pub, I hardly ever come in here.' This evening he'd had half an hour to kill; he'd come in out of the wind and rain only a few minutes earlier.

She thrust the photos at him, undeterred. 'There's no special connection with this pub. You might have seen her somewhere else in Cannonbridge, I'm just trying to trace her. I'm going to ask everywhere: pubs, shops, cafés, offices, works. I've just come over from Martleigh on the train, that's the only reason I picked this pub to start with.'

He looked through the photographs, which appeared to have been taken over a period of two or three years. The girl they showed bore a strong resemblance to the girl in front of him. She had the same long black hair, the same pale skin and very dark eyes, but she was a good deal better-looking, her features less sharp, the cheekbones more delicately moulded. 'Your sister?' he asked.

She nodded. 'Of course she's older than that now. She left home four years ago, she was only sixteen when the last of those was taken. She'll be twenty-one in March.'

'Have you heard nothing from her in four years?'

'No.'

'It's a long time,' he said. 'I wouldn't get your hopes up too high. She could be anywhere by now.'

Conversation ebbed and flowed around them. He looked up at the clock; it showed five minutes to seven. In twenty minutes he was due to pick up the parents of a lad he took an interest in, a lad on probation, making a strong effort to go straight. He was going to run them up to the infirmary where the lad was recovering from pneumonia following a severe attack of influenza.

'I haven't much time,' he told her. 'I have to go in a few minutes. Have you some special reason for wanting to find your sister?'

'I must find her,' she said with force. 'There's some money involved. My aunt died before Christmas—she lived up north, we hadn't seen her for years. We had a letter from a solicitor. My aunt didn't leave a will, and it seems my sister and I are the only relatives, her money will all come to us. Not that she had a lot to leave, a few thousand pounds, but it would mean a great deal to me. I went up north to see the solicitor. I explained about Helen, that we didn't know where she was. They won't pay the money out till she's found—or at least they will in the end, but it would take ages, and I don't want to wait for the money.'

'You need it in a hurry?'

'Yes, I do. I want to go abroad.'

'For a holiday?'

'No. To study art, in France and Italy. I never thought I'd get the chance.'

'We?' he queried. 'You said just now: We didn't know where she was.'

'I live with my stepbrother.' She pulled a face. 'I can't wait to get away.'

'He's older than you?'

'Oh yes, he's turned forty. He's as mean as sin. I'd have to wait one hell of a long time if I waited for him to give—or even lend—me the money to go abroad.'

'What's his attitude to all this? Did he encourage you to come over here to look for your sister?'

'He certainly did not. He told me I was a fool, I was wasting my time.'

'Do you definitely know that your sister came to Cannonbridge when she left home?'

'No, I don't know that. I have no idea where she went, she
didn't tell me anything. I only knew she was leaving because
I happened to go into her bedroom the evening before she left
and found her packing. I was only a kid at the time, thirteen,
and we'd never been very close. She wouldn't say where she
was going or what she was planning to do. She told me I
could have any things she left behind, she wouldn't be
coming back for them. She said: You want to clear out
yourself when you're old enough.' She laughed. 'That's what
I'm trying to do.'

'Did your stepbrother ever try to find your sister?'

'Not he. He was glad to see the back of her. He wouldn't
care if he never clapped eyes on either of us again.'

'What made you decide on Cannonbridge to start looking
for her?'

'A girl I know, a girl from school, she told me about a year
after Helen left that she'd seen her in Cannonbridge one
Saturday when she was over here shopping with her mother.
She saw Helen coming out of a café. She didn't speak to her
but she got a good look at her. She was quite certain it was
Helen.'

'Helen what?' Lambert asked.

'Mowbray. I'm Joanne Mowbray.' Her look altered suddenly, became wary, tinged with incipient hostility. 'Are you
a copper?'

'Yes.' There was a brief silence. 'I have to pick up some
people,' he said. 'I can't keep them waiting. Your best
chance is to call in at a police station. They'll do what they
can to help you.'

She set her jaw. 'I don't want the police dragged into this.
And I'm sure Helen wouldn't either.' She picked up the
photographs. 'If she's here I'll find her. She took a secretarial
and book-keeping course at school, she worked for an agency
before she left Martleigh. I'll call in at the agencies here in
the morning, she could have gone to one of them.'

'I'm at the main police station here in Cannonbridge,' he

told her. 'My name's Lambert. Detective-Sergeant Lambert. If you call in there tomorrow morning—' She was already shaking her head. 'It doesn't have to be me,' he added. 'You can see someone else—or you can call in at one of the other stations if you prefer. I'm sure you'd find it useful.'

'No, thanks,' she said stubbornly. 'I'll manage on my own.' Without looking at him she added, 'Thanks, anyway, for taking the time to talk to me.' She glanced up and flashed him a sudden smile. She had small, even teeth, very white; she looked all at once open and vulnerable, scarcely more than a schoolgirl. 'At least you showed more interest than the barman.'

March came in with a whirl of sleet and snow. The weather kept up its manic mood: gale force winds, showers of hail, sudden mild sweet days vanishing abruptly twenty-four hours later in fog and rain. Sergeant Lambert was kept pretty busy, no one case of consuming interest, just the steady unrelenting pressure of the old faithfuls: breaking and entering, thefts from cars, vandalism and hooliganism, minor fraud and embezzlement, assault and violence of greater or lesser degree.

On one of his sorties he found himself driving past the Railway Tavern. He had a brief surge of memory: the black-haired girl flinging back the hood of her anorak, scattering raindrops, glancing determinedly around the bar. Joanne Mowbray. If she'd called in at the main police station she certainly hadn't come his way. She might have found her sister by now; it was three weeks since that Sunday evening. The lad had left hospital, was convalescing at home with his parents.

At the thought he glanced at his watch. He might take five minutes to look in on them while he was over this way. He turned left at the next intersection. The memory of Joanne and her bundle of photographs dropped away into the recesses of his brain.

★

The Easter break threatened to be bitterly cold; night frosts, daytime temperatures kept low by brisk north-westerly winds. The evening of Good Friday was dark and overcast. At about eight o'clock a twelve-year-old lad by the name of Graham Cooney, living on the Parkfield council estate on the southern edge of Cannonbridge, a run-down area well represented in local petty-crime statistics, phoned the main police station from a call-box—to do this he had to run a quarter of a mile, all the Parkfield kiosks being, as usual, vandalized and out of action—to report the fact that his brother Jason, a child of four, had not come home since leaving the house at two in the afternoon to play with other children on the estate.

Mrs Cooney had not become seriously alarmed until the early evening. She had then sent her daughter, a girl of eight, chasing and calling round the estate, knocking on doors, asking if anyone had seen Jason. All without success. At about seven o'clock Graham had returned home and joined in the search. When he could discover no trace of the missing child it was he who had taken the decision to ring the police.

This was a routine matter for the uniformed branch. The usual drill went into operation, with some added drive because of the sharp frost forecast: patrol cars asked to keep a look-out, detailed tours of the area, broadcasts from the local radio station, asking householders to search cellars and outhouses. None of it produced any result.

At first light a more thorough and urgent search began. A troop of Scouts undertook a yard-by-yard sweep of neighbouring woodland, police cadets examined the area around the railway line and along the banks of the river. Another sharp frost was forecast for Saturday night. It was thought unlikely that a child of that age, in the clothes he was wearing when he left home, would survive a second night of hunger in the open.

By nightfall, again with no result, the Parkfield estate was alive with rumours: strange cars had been observed cruising about the streets earlier in the week; a lorry that had broken down on the main road near the entrance to the estate, on the afternoon of Good Friday, had remained stranded there until five or six in the evening. There was by now a general belief on the part of the estate dwellers—if not yet of the police— that the child had been abducted. Shortly after nine p.m. the CID were called in.

The light-bulb centred above the table in Mrs Cooney's kitchen shone down white and harsh, without the benefit of any softening shade. An ancient alarm clock on the mantel-shelf showed ten-fifteen. The house was very cold and smelled of damp and mould, with an overlay of soot. Through the party-wall came the sound of a radio, a brass band playing a rousing regimental march.

Mrs Cooney stood by the stove, making yet another pot of tea. She upturned the tea-caddy, shaking the last few leaves into the pot. She was a widow, a big, fleshy woman a year or two past forty, with a weary, resigned face, muddy skin, lifeless hair taken back anyhow, looks gone long ago from work, worry and hard times, the summit of her endeavours now, as far as personal appearances went, being merely to keep herself and her four children reasonably clean, not to drop so far down the scale of clothing as to be taken for gipsies.

'Run next door,' she instructed Graham, who was sitting hunched over the table, doing his best to keep awake, digging his knuckles into his eyes. 'Ask them if they can spare me a packet of tea. I'll let them have it back for sure on Wednes-day.' Her two other children, girls of eight and two, were upstairs in bed—the same bed, for warmth. Her husband had died six months before the youngest child was born; a strongly built, jovial man, struck suddenly down by virus pneumonia. He had been a plasterer, unemployed during the recession, finally taking the plunge and setting up on his own. He was just beginning to find his feet when he fell ill. With his death there had been an abrupt descent into poverty.

Graham pushed back his chair and went yawning out through the back door. A sturdy boy, tall for his age, with a sensible, serious air.

'He's a good lad,' Mrs Cooney observed to Sergeant Lambert who stood leaning against the dresser. 'He'd do anything for anyone. You couldn't wish for a better son.' She showed no sign of hysteria. She hadn't collapsed into tears or exhaustion, she went soldiering on through this crisis as she'd soldiered on through all the others. It seemed to Lambert that already she more than half accepted the possibility that Jason might not be found alive. She seemed to have armoured herself with a stoical, fatalistic view of life, as if she had long ago concluded that beyond a certain point struggle was useless.

She took Lambert's mug and poured in a little milk made from powdered skim; it had grown progressively more diluted as the day advanced. She poured out the tea. Just as well he didn't take sugar, her supply of that had run out some time ago.

Lambert drank his tea. 'Not a lot more we can do tonight,' he told her. 'We'll be back first thing in the morning.'

'Thank God I don't have to go to work tomorrow,' she said with fervour. Missing child or not, the loss of a few hours' wages would have been disastrous. She worked five mornings a week, five o'clock till seven, cleaning in a factory on the industrial estate. She left the two older children in charge of the little ones. She was always back by half past seven, had taught herself not to worry about them while she was away. She couldn't take a regular daytime job, not with Jason and the baby.

Graham came back with the packet of tea and set it down by the stove; he could scarcely keep his eyes open. 'You're sure you didn't see anything of Jason yesterday afternoon?'

Lambert suddenly asked him. He'd already questioned the boy. He seemed a decent enough lad, cooperative and observant, but Lambert hadn't been one hundred per cent satisfied with his answers. Nothing he could put a finger on but some doubt registered with him all the same.

Graham shook his head in silence. A gigantic yawn rose in his throat. He closed his eyes and let the yawn swell to its full gaping conclusion. 'Where were you until seven o'clock yesterday evening?' Lambert asked him.

Mrs Cooney put a hand on Graham's arm. 'You'd better get off to bed. You're asleep on your feet.' She steered him towards the door leading into the hall. She flicked a remonstrative glance at Lambert. 'He was out playing with his mates. He's told you that twice already, I don't know why you keep on asking. They were over in the woods, the other side of the railway line.'

'On a cold dark evening like that?'

'Lads don't mind a bit of weather.' She stood in the doorway, watching Graham stumble up the stairs. She came back into the kitchen, walking slowly and heavily. Her bare feet were thrust into battered old shoes; the skin of her legs, shiny, bluish white, was knotted and corded with varicose veins.

Lambert finished his tea and set down his mug. 'If there's any of them out there wanting tea,' she told him, 'send them in. I won't be going to bed just yet.'

'Try not to worry,' Lambert advised her. 'Try to get some sleep. We'll be bringing the troops in in the morning. They'll be able to cover a much wider area.' As he turned to the door a picture on the wall caught his eye: a country garden, romantically pretty, beds of hyacinths and tulips, a cat curled up asleep on the cottage window-sill. A snapshot was stuck in the side of the frame: Mrs Cooney and her husband, taken years ago on a summer holiday, Mrs Cooney tall and slim, her husband's arm around her shoulders, her head thrown back in laughter, the sea breeze blowing the skirts of her cotton dress against her beautiful, long, shapely legs.

Easter Sunday dawned bitterly cold but by seven the mists had vanished from along the river and a brilliant sun had broken through. Already the first holiday traffic was on the move. In a field beside the motorway, six miles to the south-west of Cannonbridge, a small party of troops was searching a derelict house, Stoneleigh, the property of an old man who had died years ago, leaving everything to his only living relative, a cousin in South America, who had himself died shortly afterwards.

There had been endless legal wrangles about the ownership of the property. A local farmer had made fruitless attempts to buy the land but eventually, with the coming of the motorway, he had lost interest. Once in a way someone asked a question on the local council but nothing was ever done, nothing ever resolved. Stoneleigh was gradually forgotten, sliding from the consciousness of councillors, solicitors, estate agents; no one concerned himself about it any more.

And all the while the wind and weather had been about their work. What had once been a pleasant enough four-square, dwelling was now a crumbling rain, roofless and eyeless, invaded by weeds and saplings.

'Nothing up here,' one of the soldiers called to the corporal as he came gingerly down what remained of the rotting staircase.

The party moved out into the sparkling sunshine. The corporal glanced round the field. In one corner, under overhanging bushes, he could see the end of what looked like a shed or hen-house. He jerked his head at it. 'Better take a look over there.' Two men crossed the field and parted the bushes. The corporal stood surveying the terrain, deciding on his next move.

The structure appeared to be some kind of ancient privy. A

couple of boards—considerably newer than the rest of the timber—had been placed in position at the top and bottom of the door, had been firmly secured by brass screws. The two men exchanged a glance. One of them stooped and pushed his way under the bushes, round to the back of the shed. Here there was a tiny window set high up, with a single deeply-grimed pane. He glanced about for something to break the glass and came upon a mossy half-brick. His mate joined him as he smashed in the pane. Together they peered in.

The first man wrinkled his nose at the smell that greeted him: age and decay, with some more disagreeable overlay. Inside the privy were three long bags of heavy translucent plastic, bundled close together in the confined space. Two bags were propped against the end walls, the third was squashed down on the floor; all three were tied at the mouth with stout cord. The bag on the floor was crammed with a miscellany of articles; he could see cushions, paperback books, the stiff sleeves of gramophone records.

'God Almighty!' he said suddenly. Through the plastic of the bag on the right he could make out the shape of a body, sideways on, in a green jacket and black trousers. Spilling out of the jacket hood was a tress of long dark hair.

His mate uttered an exclamation; he shifted his gaze to the bag on the left. Inside it, pressed up against the plastic, he could see locks of black hair, and, half visible through the strands, something that might once have been a face.

Half an hour later, in a hamlet no more than two miles from the Parkfield council estate, an elderly cottager living alone made his way stiffly to the far end of his garden, reluctantly driven by the bright spring sunshine to open his shed after the winter, look out his tools, make a start on the vegetable plot.

He creaked open the shed door and stood arrested, staring down, a hand up to his mouth.

Inside the shed, bedded cosily in a nest of old sacks and

newspapers, fast asleep and none the worse for his adven-
ture, lay Jason Cooney, one hand tightly clutching a bag of
sweets.

CHAPTER 2

Detective Chief Inspector Kelsey stood inside the screened-
off area of the field at Stoneleigh, talking to Sergeant
Lambert. The Chief was a big, solidly built man with
craggy features and a large, squashy nose; he had shrewd
green eyes and a crop of freckles, a head of thickly springing
carroty-red hair. He glanced at his watch and then at the
privy, both ends of which had now been removed. Nothing
more they could do at the moment, not until the entomologist, an enthusiastic little man plucked at intervals from
retirement to assist the police, had finished his examination.

Little doubt about the identity of the bodies. 'Joanne
Mowbray,' Sergeant Lambert had told the Chief a few
minutes after he arrived on the scene. 'It's more than likely
that the other one will be her sister Helen.'

The entomologist was finished at last. He came out of the
privy and crossed over to where the two men stood. The
Chief listened to what he had to say with his head bent,
looking down at the bright spring grass, displaying no sign of
unease. Sergeant Lambert felt nausea rise inside him; there
were still these pockets of squeamishness which in spite of
experience lingered on to inconvenience and embarrass him.
He managed well enough while the entomologist spoke of soil
structure and condition, moisture and desiccation, heat and
cold, the effects of stability or fluctuation in all these factors,
the less than airtight securing of the bags, but his brain
attempted to switch itself off as soon as the little man began a
lively account of the relentless, unwavering progression of
insect life, blow flies, cheese flies, flesh flies, coffin flies,

refusing to steady itself again until the expert's tone took on a conclusive note.

'As far as the older girl is concerned,' he said judicially, 'I would say her body has been in the shed between two and two and a half years. And the younger girl, four to five weeks.'

An hour or so later the sound of holiday traffic had increased, there was a constant whir and thunder from the motorway. Kelsey stood drinking a mug of scalding coffee. He had refused a sandwich, he could never fancy eating anything in circumstances such as these, however empty his stomach grew, however loud its rumblings.

The photographers had finished their work and left; the two bodies had gone off to the mortuary. The contents of each plastic bag, still kept separate, had been set out on the ground and given a preliminary examination before being taken off to the Forensic Science laboratory.

The identity of both girls had been amply confirmed from this brief scrutiny of their belongings. Joanne's National Savings bank-book was among the orderly contents of her duffel-bag, which had been stuffed in alongside her body. The book gave her home address in Martleigh: 34 Thirlstane Street. The account showed a balance of almost a hundred and ninety pounds, the last entry being a withdrawal of thirty pounds from a Cannonbridge sub post office on Tuesday, March 1st. There was over ten pounds in notes and coins in a zipped pocket of the anorak she was wearing. There was no diary, no personal letter, among the possessions of either girl.

Helen Mowbray's belongings were far more numerous than Joanne's. Inside the privy, behind the two propped-up plastic bags, they had found two suitcases of quite good quality, together with a soft, zipped handgrip. These contained clothing and various business papers; all three cases clearly belonged to Helen. Their contents had been neatly packed and were apparently undisturbed. In marked contrast to this orderliness, the rest of Helen's possessions had been tumbled pell-mell into the plastic bag that had lain on the privy floor. They undoubtedly belonged to her; her name appeared on the flyleaf of several paperbacks and on the sleeves of some of the gramophone records. Among these belongings was a shoulder-bag containing over a hundred pounds. Several articles had suffered minor damage, breakage, chipping, or tearing.

'It looks as if Helen packed the two suitcases and the handgrip herself,' Chief Inspector Kelsey said to Sergeant Lambert as they drank their coffee. 'Ready to leave for some destination. Able to take her time about it, do the job properly. Then she also had all the other stuff to take with her, all her awkwardly-shaped possessions, difficult to pack neatly into cases. It looks as if she could have been expecting someone to call for her in a vehicle and she intended stacking these loose oddments in the boot or the back of the vehicle. Then whoever it was brought along a plastic bag and just shoved the things into it anyhow, in a tearing hurry.' He chewed the inside of his cheek. 'Her cases were so neatly packed, I can't see her flinging the stuff into the bag in that careless fashion herself—or standing idly by and allowing someone else to treat her belongings in that way.'

He finished his coffee. 'No doubt about it, both murders were committed by the same man. Clearly the second girl was killed because she came along asking questions about the first. She had either stumbled on or was about to stumble on the man who had killed her sister.'

'The man?' Lambert echoed.

Kelsey thrust out his lips. 'Man or woman.' He agreed with the doctor's opinion that it could have been either. Both girls were short and slight. Both had been strangled from behind with a length of strong cord identical with that used to fasten the mouths of the plastic bags; both ligatures were still in place round the girls' necks. 'Nothing beyond the

strength of any ordinarily healthy and active woman,'
Kelsey added. 'All that was needed was a vehicle. And the
ability to use a screwdriver.'

The town of Martleigh was a good deal smaller than
Cannonbridge and lay twenty-two miles to the north-east. 34
Thirlstane Street proved to be a small butcher's shop standing at the end of an Edwardian terrace in a respectable
working-class district a mile or so from the town centre.
There were no front gardens; the houses opened directly on
to the street. When Sergeant Lambert halted the car and
stepped out on to the pavement there were only the peaceful
sounds of Sunday morning to be heard under the pale blue
sky: radio music, children playing in a nearby street, a dog
barking, the hum of traffic, a woman calling a child.

Gilded letters above the shop read: A. F. LOCKYEAR.
FAMILY BUTCHER. The marble display slabs in the window
had been washed down with scrupulous care; behind them a
precise row of sheaves of white greaseproof paper, neatly
impaled on metal hooks, obscured any view of the interior.
Kelsey got out of the car and glanced up at the living
quarters. The curtains were drawn back but there was no
sign of life.

Sergeant Lambert pressed the doorbell. After a minute or
two when there was no answer he pressed the bell again,
keeping his finger on it for several seconds. Still no reply. He
was about to press it for the third time when he became
aware of someone watching from the house next door. A
whisk of movement behind the net curtains of the downstairs
window, a hand lifting the curtain discreetly to one side, a
woman's face appearing briefly at the other side of the glass.
He stood waiting for her front door to open, as it did a few
moments later.

A little birdlike woman of fifty or so came out on to the
doorstep. She wore a trim nylon overall, her brown hair was
neatly and becomingly dressed. She gave both men rapid

up-and-down glances from her bright black boot-button
eyes. She darted a swift look at the car before she spoke,
knowing them at once for policemen.

'Something wrong?' She stepped out on to the pavement.
When Kelsey didn't answer she added, 'Mr Lockyear's not
here. There's no one at home. He's on his own just now, with
Joanne being away. I could take a message.'

'Perhaps you could tell us where we could find Mr
Lockyear?' Kelsey said.

'He's down at his allotment. He's always there this time of
a Sunday, Easter or no Easter, makes no difference. He won't
get back here till just before one, all he'll do is cook himself a
chop.' A mouth-watering odour of roasting turkey, sage and
onion stuffing, drifted out behind her. Lambert felt all at
once acutely hungry. 'Is there something wrong?' she asked
again with the same lively, inquisitive air.

Kelsey still didn't answer that. 'Where can we find these
allotments?' he asked.

She gave him directions. 'You've been very helpful,' he
told her. 'Very good of you, Mrs—'

'Mrs Snape,' she said at once. 'If there's anything I can
do—'

'Thank you,' he said, with finality. They went back to the
car. She remained standing on the pavement, watching them
with unabashed curiosity. 'You can get back here tomorrow,'
Kelsey told Lambert as the car moved off. 'She'll talk her
head off, given half a chance.'

The allotments were some three-quarters of a mile away, on
the northern tip of Martleigh, in an open, windswept situation. The air was full of the cries of domestic fowl mingled
with the chirruping of songbirds. Somewhere a radio played
a Strauss waltz. Judging from the lingering, acrid smell
as they crossed the bleak terrain, someone had recently
cleaned out the fowl pens, had scattered the manure over
the earth.

There was no great air of urgency about the place. Twelve or fourteen men, middle-aged or older, dug and planted in a leisurely fashion. Kelsey asked the first man they encountered if he could point out Mr Lockyear to them. 'Arnold Lockyear?' the man said. He gestured with an earth-stained hand. 'He's over there, at the far end.'

Lockyear had his back to them as they came over. He was stooping over a bed of rhubarb, examining the crowns, replacing ancient bottomless buckets and wooden orange boxes over the slender stalks. The other men continued to work on their plots, displaying no open curiosity.

Lockyear turned his head at the sound of their approach. He paused in his task and then straightened up. He remained where he was, in silence, his face expressionless, his eyes darting over them in swift assessment.

'Arnold Lockyear?' the Chief said. Lockyear gave a single nod. His face wore the look of a man who knows with certainty that he is about to hear bad news. A short, stocky man within hailing distance of middle age; a thick red neck and fleshy, jowled face, deepset brown eyes, thickly curling hair the colour of a cobnut. He looked not unlike a yearling bull.

The Chief identified himself and Lambert. The look on Lockyear's face intensified, he closed his eyes for an instant.

'I'm afraid we have bad news,' Kelsey said. 'Very bad news.' The manure-scented breeze blew in their faces. From the neighbouring allotments the thock and click of tools sounded clear and distinct on the shimmering air.

'It's Joanne,' Lockyear said with grim certainty. He stood with bowed head as the Chief said what had to be said. As he listened his face took on a look of stunned disbelief. When the Chief came to the end of his harrowing recital Lockyear raised his eyes and stared into Kelsey's face. An expression of horror overlaid with frowning questioning appeared on his blunt features.

There was a brief silence, then Lockyear said with an air of frozen shock, 'Both of them? Both the girls? Helen as well?'

'I'm afraid so,' the Chief said gently.

Lockyear drew a long quavering breath. He shook his head as if trying to clear it. 'Let me get this straight,' he said in a dogged way as if it might all somehow turn out to be no more than a piece of lunatic misunderstanding. 'There's no possible doubt about it? Both the girls are dead?'

'I'm afraid there's no doubt at all,' Kelsey said. 'They're both dead.' Lockyear stood looking at him with his arms hanging limply at his sides.

'I'm afraid I must ask you to carry out an unpleasant duty,' Kelsey said. Lockyear gave him an uncomprehending look. 'I must ask you to come with us to the Cannonbridge mortuary, to identify the bodies.'

Lockyear's mouth opened a little. He turned his head and stared down at the rhubarb crowns with their delicate rosy stems tipped with pale yellow leaves, frilled and crimped. He gave a single nod.

'And we'll need to ask you some questions,' Kelsey said. 'I'm sure you understand that. When you last saw the girls, what contacts you may have had with them since that time, who their friends and associates were, and so on. Any light you can throw on what's happened. It will all take time, as I'm sure you'll appreciate.'

Lockyear nodded slowly, he went on nodding for some seconds.

'The post mortem will take place tomorrow morning,' Kelsey said. Lockyear gave another slow, bemused series of nods. 'You'll probably want to call in at your house before we go to Cannonbridge,' Kelsey added as Lockyear continued to stand there. 'You may want to change your clothes, there may be something you need to see to. We can wait while you attend to it.'

Lockyear glanced down at his clothes. 'Yes, I suppose I'd better change.' He looked vaguely about. 'I'd better clear up here.' He covered the rest of the rhubarb, gathered up his

fork and spade, trowel and hoe, without haste. He put them
tidily away in the shed and locked the door, testing it
afterwards to see that it was properly secured. All his actions
were marked with care and deliberation, though his face still
wore its drained, numbed look.

He didn't speak to any of the other men working on the
allotments as he walked away beside the two policemen; the
men continued with their digging and forking as if unaware
of the little party making its way past them. But when they
reached the car and Lambert glanced back he saw that they
had all now stopped working and were openly staring after
them.

The drive to Thirlstane Street took place in silence. When
they reached Lockyear's shop it was lunch-time and the
street was deserted. Lockyear was able to dart into his house
unnoticed. The two men followed him inside. The air smelt
stale and musty as if no one bothered to open the windows
any more.

'I'd like to take a look in Joanne's room,' Kelsey told
Lockyear. 'You can carry on with whatever you have to do.'

Lockyear led the way upstairs and opened a door on the
right of the landing. 'This is Joanne's room,' he said. 'Helen
had the room next door—it hasn't been used since she left.'
He went off along the corridor to the bathroom.

Kelsey went into Joanne's room and looked swiftly
through her belongings. The room was adequately furnished, reasonably comfortable. All the soft furnishings
looked in need of repair or renewal, as if nothing much in that
line had been done for several years.

Joanne's clothes were neatly arranged in a single wardrobe and a chest of drawers. Not a great deal of clothing and
nothing very fancy; plain, functional, inexpensive garments.
Beside the window stood a small bureau; none of the drawers
was locked. The top drawer held an assortment of papers,
methodically disposed. The letter from the aunt's solicitor. A
bundle of school reports: Joanne had been an industrious

pupil, usually first in form at Art. Well behaved, presenting no problems; otherwise unremarkable. Photographs and snapshots, going back over a number of years, all with carefully written identifications. A wedding photograph of her parents, the bridegroom a resolute-looking young man, tall and slightly built, with a good forehead; the bride short and slight with a delicate, pretty face and shy smile, a great deal of dark hair dressed in curls and loops under her filmy veil.

A second wedding photograph, taken nine years after the first: the marriage of the girls' mother to Arnold Lockyear's father, the bridegroom grey-haired and bull-necked, with no discernible waistline but with a cheerful, good-tempered face alight with pride and love. His hand clasped the hand of his bride, even more slender and delicate-looking now in a dress and jacket of pale silk, a pretty little veiled cloche hat perched on her dark hair, still abundant, still glossy and wavy. She had an air of having passed through some harsh weathering process since she had last taken the arm of a bridegroom; the look was temporarily overlaid with an expression of tenuous optimism.

In front of the bridal pair stood two little girls in long dresses of Victorian print, their dark hair taken back under ribboned head-dresses, their hands clutching formal posies. Helen half a head taller than Joanne, both of them with ritual smiles fixed over an air of uncertainty.

Arnold Lockyear stood beside his father, with a space of a good couple of feet between them as if he had been determined to mark out the distance separating him from the rest of the family group. He wore a dark suit, a carnation prinked with greenery in his buttonhole; he looked straight ahead, his expression blank and unsmiling.

In the second drawer of the bureau were some paper-backed books: lives of various artists and a history of European art; a number of postcard-size reproductions of famous paintings; some copies of magazines devoted to the

arts. And a portfolio of drawings and watercolours, all dated
and signed: Joanne E. Mowbray, in a hand that grew
progressively less rounded and childish as Kelsey turned the
pages. Careful pencil studies of faces, animals, buildings;
landscapes and townscapes in line and wash; heads of children in crayon and pastel. They looked competent enough to
Kelsey; he wouldn't have minded half a dozen on the walls
of his flat.

In the lowest drawer he found a handful of trinkets, a few
pressed flowers, some carefully preserved lengths of satin
ribbon decorated with bows, such as might have been used to
tie up presents. More photographs: Lockyear senior and his
second wife with the two girls on a seaside holiday, all
apparently enjoying themselves; Lockyear lying back in a
deckchair with a straw hat shading his eyes, Joanne kneeling
beside her mother's chair, talking of her, both of them
looking relaxed and carefree, Helen sitting beside them on
the sand, absorbed in a book.

Kelsey closed the drawer and went next door into Helen's
room. Dusty sunlight streamed through the panes. A butter-
fly lay shrivelled on the window-ledge. The bed had been
stripped, the mattress covered with an old cotton bedspread.
The walls were bare, the wardrobe and chest of drawers
empty except for a yellowed lining of newspapers bearing a
date some five years ago. In the top drawer of the dressing-
table, under the lining, were a few blue beads and a torn
piece of pink face tissue. In one of the small drawers was a
child's ring with a stone of red glass, and a motto from a
Christmas cracker. Kelsey came out of the room and closed
the door. He went slowly downstairs.

Sergeant Lambert was standing waiting in the hall; Lockyear was in the kitchen. He had washed, had changed into a
dark suit and white shirt. He poured himself a cup of milk
from the fridge. He held up the bottle and glanced at the
Chief but Kelsey shook his head. 'Ready when you are,' he
said.

Lockyear drained the milk in a single gulp. He washed his cup, locked up, and followed the two men out to the car.

He took his seat beside Kelsey in the rear. He made no attempt at conversation but kept his head averted, his elbow resting against the window, the outspread fingers supporting his forehead. After some little time Kelsey became aware that he was crying. The holiday traffic streamed towards them, family parties with excited children laughing and waving, dogs staring out through rear windows, blasts of music from radios as the cars swept past.

Some minutes later Lockyear drew a shuddering sigh. He sat up and took a handkerchief from his pocket. He dried his eyes, dabbed at his cheeks. He put the handkerchief away, drew several more trembling breaths and then fell silent. After a brief interval he said in a detached, explanatory tone. 'They were both wilful, stubborn girls. There was no doing anything with them.' Neither Kelsey nor Lambert made any reply.

Another minute or two slipped by, then Lockyear said, 'I don't suppose I understood either of them.' He sounded as if he no longer expected any response but was simply expressing his thoughts aloud. 'Hardly likely, I suppose, me being a bachelor.' He said nothing more but sat in silence until the car halted outside the Cannonbridge mortuary.

Lambert got out and opened the car doors. Kelsey stepped out on to the forecourt but Lockyear didn't budge. Lambert stooped and glanced in at him; he seemed to be making an effort to compose himself. Lambert said nothing but continued to look in at him. Lockyear suddenly jerked himself up and out of the car. He stood bracing his shoulders, drawing deep breaths, looking straight ahead.

'Right then!' he said with an attempt at briskness. 'Let's get it over with.'

When they came out into the mortuary corridor a few minutes later Lockyear was very pale. Tears ran down his

face but he appeared unaware of them. He stood stranded in
the middle of the corridor; he seemed at a total loss. Lambert
put a hand under his elbow and steered him out of the
building, down the steps, towards the car.

The Chief took his seat again in the back beside Lockyear.
As the car pulled out Lockyear suddenly said, 'This will
finish me. It'll ruin the business. I know it.' He dropped his
head into his hands.

'I should have a word with your doctor when you get back
to Martleigh,' Kelsey said.

Lockyear made no reply. They reached an intersection
and Lambert turned the car in the direction of the main
police station.

CHAPTER 3

Very little time elapsed between the local radio station's
broadcast of the news that Jason Cooney had been found safe
and well and its first news flash of the discovery at Stoneleigh
of the bodies of two young women. After the police had
broken the news to Arnold Lockyear the radio station made
further broadcasts, giving details of the two girls. Shortly
afterwards the phone calls began to come in.

Among the hoaxers and the nutters were several genuine
calls; the more important of these the Chief intended to deal
with himself. His first call, a little after eight on Monday
morning, was on a Mrs Huband, the landlady with whom
Joanne Mowbray had lodged during her brief stay in
Cannonbridge; Mrs Huband lived in a terrace close to the
railway station.

She was outside, perched on a stepladder, busily cleaning
her windows, when they arrived. A plump, motherly-looking
woman in late middle age, greying hair twisted into a bun;
her print overall was carefully laundered. She abandoned

her bucket and wash-leather and took the two men into her
spotlessly clean little house.

'I was that upset when I heard it over the radio,' she
told the Chief, her eyes filled with distress. 'I'd often
wondered how Joanne had got on, if she'd managed to find
her sister.'

She had had no other lodger during the few days Joanne
had stayed with her. 'She found it quite comfortable here,
and quite convenient, but she couldn't afford to stay more
than a few days.' She looked earnestly up at him. 'It's not
that I charge a lot, I wouldn't want you to think that, but it's
all I have to live on, that and the widow's pension.' She
pressed her hands together. 'Anyway, she said she had to be
careful with her money, so I told her about the girls' hostel. I
advised her to go along there and see the Warden.' The
hostel was an old-established concern in a residential quarter
of Cannonbridge, run by a charitable trust.

Kelsey asked if she knew what success Joanne had had in
her inquiries about her sister.

'At first she was very pleased with what she'd been able to
find out,' Mrs Huband said. 'She thought she was making
good progress.' She'd been along to two secretarial agencies
Helen had worked for and she'd made contact with other
people who had known Helen or employed her services. 'But
on the Wednesday morning I could see she was looking a bit
down in the mouth. It seemed that everyone she'd come
across who'd known Helen had known her some time ago,
she hadn't been able to find anyone who'd known her
recently. She was beginning to think Helen must have left
this area. She was in two minds about staying on in Cannonbridge at all, she thought she could be wasting her time—and
her money. Perhaps she should give up and go back to
Martleigh. It depended what she found out that day.'

Joanne had been along to the hostel on the Tuesday
afternoon to explain her position. The Warden had told her
she could have a bed there any night as long as she let them

know before seven-thirty in the evening; if it was later than that, then she would have to take her chance. 'So she squared up with me on the Wednesday morning,' Mrs Huband said. 'She told me she'd call back for her things about four o'clock. I said not to be later than four because I had to go out— I help at the Darby and Joan club on Wednesdays.' She drew a sighing breath. 'She was a nice girl, not pushy or inconsiderate, though she was very determined.'

'Was she back by four?'

'Yes, she came in about ten to.'

'Did you speak to her?'

'I didn't have much time, I had to rush off. I told her to make herself a cup of tea, and to be sure to drop the latch when she left. She was the sort you could go off and leave in the house without worrying about what she might get up to. She was as honest as the day. You can always tell.'

'Did she tell you how she'd got on that day? If she'd decided what she was going to do?'

'I asked her if she'd had any luck. She just said: Nothing special. She still hadn't made up her mind about going back to Martleigh that evening. She said she had another two or three leads to follow up, she'd be going after them in the next hour or two, then she'd make up her mind.'

'How had she done her hair that day?'

She looked startled at the sudden switch. 'The same as every other day, just long and straight.'

'Did she ever wear anything in her hair? A ribbon or a comb, perhaps?' Caught up in the tresses of Joanne's long dark hair was a large decorative hairslide with the catch open. The slide was of heavy quality polystyrene, white veined with green; it had a fancy curved top

Mrs Huband shook her head. 'I never saw her wear anything in her hair.'

'What time did you get back home that Wednesday evening?'

'About ten o'clock. She'd taken all her things—she only

had the one bag with her, a duffel-bag. She'd left everything nice and tidy, the house properly locked up.'

When they left Mrs Huband's they went straight along to the hostel but the Warden could tell them nothing further. Helen Mowbray had never had any contact with the hostel and Joanne had neither shown up again or phoned, after her visit on the Tuesday afternoon. Nor had she mentioned, during that visit, the names of any contacts she hoped to see the following day.

They called next on a Miss Gallimore who had phoned the station to say that Helen Mowbray had at one time lodged with her. Miss Gallimore was an old woman, white-haired and fresh-complexioned, with an air of having seen better days; she lived in a run-of-the-mill red-brick semi in a side street not far from the centre of town. She took them into a sitting-room with a great many faded family photographs in ornate old frames ranged on top of the piano and along the mantelshelf.

Helen had come to lodge with her almost exactly four years ago, when she had first come to Cannonbridge. She had been the sole lodger; Miss Gallimore never took more than one girl at a time. Helen had stayed about a year; thirteen months, to be precise. She had been a very satisfactory lodger, always paying promptly, clean and tidy, pleasant and polite, quiet and hard-working.

Miss Gallimore's recollection was that Helen had worked for agencies when she first came to lodge with her, then she had had one or two spells of working for a particular employer, with some freelancing in between. She was able to give them the names of two employers: the Cannonbridge branch of Wyatt Fashions, and Fletcher's Plastics, on the industrial estate.

Kelsey asked her if Helen had had any men friends. Yes, she had, that is, she had gone out sometimes in the evenings or at weekends and Miss Gallimore had assumed it was with some man or other. She had never brought anyone to the house, had never mentioned anyone. 'I didn't ask her personal questions,' Miss Gallimore said. 'It's never been my way, and I'm sure she wouldn't have welcomed it. She wasn't a chatty girl.'

Why had Helen decided to leave after thirteen months?

'We didn't have any disagreement or anything like that. She was beginning to do quite well in her little business and she felt she could afford a place of her own. She told me she'd seen a furnished flat she liked.' Miss Gallimore hadn't seen Helen again after she left. 'I can give you the address of the flat,' she added, 'but it's not much use your going round there. The house has been pulled down, they've put up some flats there. You probably know the place—Holmwood, the house was called, on the Tappenhall Road. It had a big garden.'

Yes, Kelsey did know the place, on the southern tip of Cannonbridge. An Edwardian house had stood there until a couple of years ago. The site was occupied now by sheltered-accommodation units for the elderly.

He asked if Joanne had contacted Miss Gallimore. Yes, she had called at the house on a Monday afternoon at the end of February; she had been given the address by the Cannonbridge Secretarial Agency. Miss Gallimore had told her what she had just told the Chief. Joanne had said nothing to her about any discoveries she had made or any leads she intended following.

When they left the house Kelsey looked at his watch: time to be getting along for the results of the post mortem. The Cannonbridge Secretarial Agency would have to wait till tomorrow when the agency would be open again after the Bank Holiday, but they could call in at the Tradesmen's Agency this afternoon. This was a small concern run from a private house by a Mrs Ingram; it dealt with the services of plumbers, carpenters, electricians and the like. Mrs Ingram had phoned them on Sunday evening to say that Helen Mowbray had worked for several of the men on the agency books; she would be at home all day if they wished to talk to her. 'After we've seen her,' Kelsey told Sergeant Lambert, 'you can get on over to Martleigh again, see if you can manage a word with that neighbour of Lockyear's, Mrs Snape.'

The post mortem provided no surprises; afterwards there was a conference, briefings, the Press to be dealt with. It was turned three by the time they reached the small detached dwelling that housed the office of the Tradesmen's Agency.

Mrs Ingram was on the phone when they arrived. She was a youngish woman with a briskly capable manner. She had spent the morning attempting to contact the men on her books in order to ask them about their dealings with Helen Mowbray, but she had been able to speak to very few of them, because of the holiday. From those she had spoken to she had learned nothing of significance.

Helen had got in touch with her shortly after she arrived in Cannonbridge. Mrs Ingram had given her a list of agency members; one or two had immediately employed Helen to prepare their accounts. Her work had been excellent. She had subsequently been employed by several others on the books; there had never been any complaints.

Mrs Ingram handed the Chief a list of members with a mark against the names of those she knew had employed Helen. 'I can't imagine there was ever any question of any personal involvement with any of our members,' she said with the air of a tigress protecting her young. You'd hardly be likely to know if there was, Kelsey thought, running his eye down the list. Most of the addresses were in Cannonbridge, a few in neighbouring villages.

Yes, Joanne had contacted Mrs Ingram on the morning of Monday, February 28th. 'She phoned to ask if she could come round to see me,' Mrs Ingram said. 'I saw her at twelve o'clock.' She showed the Chief the entry in her desk diary.

She had given Joanne much the same information as she

had just given the Chief. She had later heard that Joanne had phoned every man on the agency list and had called to see two or three. 'She was certainly thorough,' she said with a note of respect. 'But as far as I know, none of them was able to tell her anything very much. None of them had had any dealings with Helen for two years or more.' It had been her private opinion that Helen had probably gone off to London or some provincial city, that Joanne didn't stand much chance of coming across any recent traces of her in Cannon-bridge.

The afternoon sun was still warm as Sergeant Lambert drove over to Martleigh; there was a welcome temporary lull in the holiday traffic.

Earlier in the afternoon Arnold Lockyear had duly tele-phoned to learn the findings of the post mortem. He had made no comment on the results, had merely confirmed that he would be attending the inquest later in the week.

According to the lengthy statement he had made on Sunday, after his visit to the mortuary, Lockyear had had no contact of any kind with Helen after she left Thirlstane Street four years ago. Nor had he had any kind of communication from Joanne since she had gone off to look for Helen at the end of February. In neither case had he expected any contact. 'I dare say you'll hear this from others,' he told the Chief, looking at him with weary resignation, 'so you might as well hear it first from me. I was never on what you would call very friendly terms with either of the girls.'

Arnold's mother had died when he was twenty, and his father had married Mrs Mowbray, a widow, seven years later; her daughters, Helen and Joanne, were at that time aged eight and four. 'I did my best to get on with them all,' Arnold told the Chief. Things had gone along well enough until the death of the second Mrs Lockyear a few years later. She was a woman of some refinement, fond of reading and music, very different from the robust, down-to-earth

countrywoman his father had married first time round. The
second Mrs Lockyear had fussed over her daughters, dressed
them in artistic clothes she made and embroidered herself,
encouraged them to think of themselves as talented, likely to
make a place for themselves in the world beyond the domestic hearth. Her new husband humoured her, charmed by
his luck in snaring this unlikely bird of paradise. Arnold was
living at home, working in the shop—he had worked there
ever since leaving school. He had felt himself an outsider in
the new family circle. It was then that he had taken on the
allotment, had begun to spend his spare time digging
and hoeing, planting and weeding, in fair weather and
foul.

Perhaps if the marriage had lasted longer Lockyear senior
might have ceased to humour his new wife to the same
extent, but three years after she walked out of the register
office on his arm she was abruptly taken off by a rapid
disorder of the blood. Her husband couldn't believe she
would die. Right up until the last moment he had fought
against the idea, had refused to countenance it. He was
knocked sideways by her death. Certainly there was never
any question of his going out to look for any successor to her.

He was determined to look after his stepdaughters with
every possible care. He went next door and asked Mrs Snape
if she would come in daily to cook and clean, keep an eye on
the domestic side of things in general, watch over the two
motherless girls. She had readily agreed.

Things continued in this fashion for another four years and
then Lockyear himself died, dropping dead from a heart
attack one afternoon as he was unloading the van after a trip
to the slaughter-house—right there in Thirlstane Street, in
front of the shop, standing by the rear doors of the van, with
Arnold helping him to unload.

After that it was just Arnold and the two girls, Helen now
almost sixteen and Joanne twelve. In Lockyear's will everything had been left to Arnold; house, business, furniture,

savings. There was a clause instructing Arnold to pay over by way of dowry the sum of three thousand pounds to each girl on the occasion of her marriage or at the age of thirty if she should still be unmarried at that time. In addition Arnold was charged with continuing to provide a home in Thirlstane Street for both girls for as long as they should require it.

'What happens to the dowry money now?' Kelsey had asked. It seemed it would pass to Arnold. Certainly not a fortune, Lambert mused, though many men had killed for a great deal less. He had no idea if Arnold was in any way strapped for cash, how well the shop was doing.

'I certainly didn't drive either of the girls out of the house,' Arnold had said with some heat. 'Whatever you may hear from others.' It was true that shortly after his father's death he had made some alterations to the way the household was run; that was surely only to be expected. He had informed Mrs Snape that her services would no longer be required. 'After all,' he told the Chief, his brown eyes steady and unflagging, 'Helen was rising sixteen. Some girls are married at that age, running a house and looking after a husband, entirely on their own. I didn't see why she shouldn't buckle down to a bit of housework. I felt it would do her good, she'd have to learn how to manage a home one day. And Joanne was old enough to help. They were both strong, healthy girls. I couldn't see that it was any great hardship.'

Helen was at that time in her final year at school, taking a course in book-keeping and secretarial skills. Kelsey asked how she had received the news that Mrs Snape would no longer be coming in to run the house. Arnold had shrugged. 'She didn't say anything, she just got on and did what was needed. She was good at it too. I wasn't surprised. I knew they learned domestic science, cookery and needlework, all that kind of thing, at school. It was just that she'd never been asked to do it before.' No, she had never appeared to resent the change, she had never made any comment. Some fifteen months later, a few days after her seventeenth birthday, she had left home.

Kelsey asked Lockyear to outline the circumstances. 'She left school in the summer,' Arnold told him. 'She'd done well there. She'd won a couple of prizes, one of them was for being the best student on the secretarial course. She could easily have got a good steady job in Martleigh right away. I know for a fact she was offered one in a solicitor's office and another with an estate agent—on account of winning the secretarial prize. But she wouldn't take either of the jobs, and she wouldn't look for another.' She hadn't discussed the matter with him. 'That wasn't her way,' he said with a note of old resentments. She had gone along to a secretarial agency in Martleigh and put herself on their books; they had sent her out to local temporary and relief jobs.

'And I also know for a fact,' Arnold had added, 'that she was offered jobs by different employers she worked for while she was with the agency.' But again she had accepted none of them. One spring morning, seven or eight months after she joined the agency, she had left home. She hadn't told him she intended going, she had left no note, had apparently said nothing to Joanne. He had only become aware that she had left when he came into the house after closing the shop for the day and had found no sign of supper and no sign of Helen. When she hadn't come in by nightfall he had gone into her bedroom and found most of her belongings gone.

'Were you surprised?' Kelsey asked. Arnold shook his head. 'No, I can't say I was. She was always secretive.' He had phoned the agency to see if they knew anything. They told him Helen had given the usual month's notice and had left with an excellent reference from them and no doubt equally good references from various employers. She had given them to understand she was taking a short holiday and then going off to some larger centre, London or one of the provincial cities, in search of wider opportunities.

Arnold hadn't worried overmuch about her, he had felt she was quite capable of looking after herself.

Joanne was then fourteen, reasonably competent in the house. She worked well at school, was no trouble there or at home. A quiet girl who never bothered with boyfriends, never wanted to go out to discos or parties. She had stayed in her room a lot, reading, studying, drawing; she hadn't appeared to miss Helen.

In due course she had left school. She had wanted to take an art course, had wanted to go off to some college near London. But it would have cost a lot of money—and Arnold couldn't see what it could lead to. The local education authority had cut back on discretionary grants and in any case didn't look with favour on art courses, taking the view that the country was already oversupplied with unemployed designers—a view Arnold heartily endorsed.

He had done his best to discourage these notions on Joanne's part. He reckoned she'd inherited her fancy ideas from her mother. 'She wanted me to advance her the money for the course,' he said. 'Out of the three thousand that would be coming to her one day under my father's will. Of course I refused. The whole of the three thousand would have been swallowed up well before the course ended—and that wasn't what my father had in mind for the money, he intended it as a nest-egg for the future.' He had told Joanne she could either find herself a job right away in the town or she could take some sensible, straightforward course at the Martleigh College of Further Education. If she didn't fancy the secretarial side there was domestic science, accountancy, hotel catering; a wide variety of practical, down-to-earth subjects.

'But she wouldn't have any of them,' he said. 'She went out and got herself a temporary job.' At an art shop in Martleigh, serving behind the counter while one of the regular girls was in hospital. The job had lasted a few weeks, then she had worked for three months in a needlework shop where one of the assistants was on maternity leave. After that she was taken on in a department store for the Christmas rush and the January sales. Shortly before her stint there came to an end the letter had arrived from the solicitor up north, informing the girls of the death of their mother's sister. Joanne had appeared very anxious to get her hands on her share of the aunt's money, but she hadn't told him she intended going to Cannonbridge to look for Helen; he had known nothing about that until the Sunday she left. She had simply informed him as she cleared away the breakfast things that she was going.

He had had no idea that she knew of anything to link Helen with Cannonbridge. She hadn't mentioned any such link to him then, she had merely told him that that was where she was going. He asked how long she intended staying. She had shrugged and told him to expect her when he saw her. She might go on somewhere else from Cannonbridge, it depended on what she found out. He had told her she was on a fool's errand, the money from the aunt's intestacy would be paid over in the end, he couldn't see why there need be so much rush.

No, he hadn't worried about her. She was as determined a character as Helen; she was intelligent and serious-minded, had always behaved sensibly in Martleigh, he had no reason to suppose she would behave otherwise in Cannonbridge.

'If you had never heard of her again,' Kelsey put to him, 'if she had simply stayed away, like Helen, would you have done anything about it?'

Arnold was silent for a minute or two. His eyes never left the Chief's face. At length he said, 'No, I don't believe I would. I'd probably have thought she'd found Helen and decided to stay with her.'

'You wouldn't have expected her to inform you of that decision?'

He shook his head. 'Probably not. I don't think you quite appreciate what self-willed, independent girls they were.'

What would happen to the aunt's money, now that both

girls were dead? 'I imagine it will all go to the State.' Arnold had looked unwaveringly at the Chief. 'It certainly won't come to me. The old lady was no kin of mine.' Hard to see how Arnold stood to benefit by the girls' deaths, Lambert pondered—apart from no longer having to pay out the two dowries.

Kelsey had asked how often Arnold had visited Cannonbridge over the last few years. 'I came here on a coach trip about fifteen years ago,' Arnold had answered. 'I haven't been here since, never had any occasion to.' He had paused briefly. 'Until today.'

CHAPTER 4

There was no sign of life in the butcher's shop or the living accommodation when Lambert reached Thirlstane Street. He got out of his car and stood surveying the property; he could discern no movement behind the windows, no sound from within.

He went next door and pressed the bell; it was a minute or two before his ring was answered. When the door was at last flung open Mrs Snape stood facing him with an expression of lively irritation that was at once replaced by a smile of welcome.

'Oh, it's you!' she exclaimed. Her dark skirt and ruffled blouse were protected by a smart frilled apron; she wore sparkling ear-rings and a matching necklace. Her hair was elaborately arranged, her face carefully made up. She came out on to the step and glanced sharply up and down the street. 'I thought it was another reporter.'

'Have they been pestering you?' Lambert asked.

She shrugged. 'It was him they wanted, of course.' She jerked her head towards No. 34. 'But he wouldn't speak to them, he wouldn't even answer the door. I told them they were wasting their time. He's an obstinate man, I said, you can ring his bell till you're blue in the face but if he's made up his mind not to come out, then come out he will not. They took some pictures of the shop.' She smiled fleetingly and touched her hair. 'They took a picture of me as well, standing here in the doorway, looking over at the shop. It'll be in all the papers. They asked me a lot of questions about Arnold and the girls, about the family in general. Of course I'm very well placed to answer. No one round here knows more about the Mowbrays and the Lockyears than I do.'

She frowned suddenly. 'What was it you were wanting? I'm up to the eyes just now. I've got my sister-in-law and her husband, and their son and his wife and family, coming over to tea in half an hour. They've been on the phone already this morning, wanting to know all about this dreadful business. I've had half the neighbourhood phoning or calling round, asking me what I know.' She spoke with a mixture of pride and irritation. 'All of a sudden I'm the most popular woman in the street.' She gave a little jerk of her head. 'Oh well— you'd better come inside. I can get on while I'm talking to you, better than standing out here doing nothing.'

He followed her into the house. She stood watching with a hawklike gaze to see that he wiped his feet properly before she allowed him to set foot on her hall carpet, brilliantly patterned in crimson and beige, a design of huge cabbage roses that made the tiny hall look even smaller.

'My husband's over at my sister-in-law's now,' she threw at him over her shoulder as she led the way into the kitchen, recently modernized, furnished with expensive-looking units, the latest model electric cooker. 'He's taking a look at their car, it's been playing them up. Never happy unless he's getting his hands dirty, my husband, even on a Bank Holiday.' She waved a hand. 'He's done all this himself.'

A large table in the centre of the kitchen was covered with plates, dishes and basins holding food in various stages of preparation: the remains of a cold turkey, a highly decorated trifle, a packet of sliced bread, a lettuce in a plastic bag, tomatoes, cucumber, hard-boiled eggs, beetroot, tins of peaches, fruit salad, cream. Whatever else awaited her in-laws, it wouldn't appear to be death from starvation.

'I gather you used to help out next door,' Lambert said. 'Until old Mr Lockyear died.'

'That's right.' She began to cut delicate slices of turkey breast. 'Mr Lockyear came round here to ask me, he made a special favour of it. I wouldn't have done it for anyone else. And it was handy, being next door. I never had any trouble from either of the girls. They were always well behaved, quiet girls, nicely brought up. I got on well with the old man too, he was very straight, very considerate. He was well liked round here, well respected.'

She glanced up at Lambert. 'His second wife was a very nice-looking woman. The chap she was married to before, he was a decent enough fellow, a commercial artist, worked for himself. They never had two pennies to rub together, they just struggled along. He had poor health, something wrong with his kidneys. He was in and out of hospital the last few years before he died. She had to give piano lessons to keep going. They lived near here, a few streets away, she always got her meat at Lockyear's.'

She turned her attention to buttering slices of bread. 'She had a hard time of it after her husband died. Joanne was only two or three years old. But she always kept the two girls very neat and clean.'

'Were you surprised when she married Lockyear?' Lambert asked.

'I was and I wasn't,' she said with a judicial purse of her lips. Lambert, who had subsisted all day on small and infrequent snacks, couldn't prevent his gaze from resting on the pale, succulent slices of turkey. She turned her head suddenly and caught his yearning eye. 'Hungry, are you?' Without waiting for an answer she picked up a couple of slices on the point of the carving knife and deposited them between slices of bread. She thrust the sandwich at him. 'Help yourself to mustard and pickle.' Lambert began to eat with gratitude and energy.

'Make yourself a cup of coffee,' she said. 'Don't bother with any for me, I haven't got the time.' She resumed her swift buttering. 'She certainly wasn't the type I'd have bet money on if I'd ever thought of old Lockyear marrying again, but afterwards, when I came to think about it, I could see it was really a very suitable match for both of them. She never had any more financial worries. He gave her a comfortable home—she'd been living in rented rooms. And he was very good to the two girls, he treated them as if they were his own.'

She paused and stared at the opposite wall. 'He worshipped the ground that woman walked on, anyone could see that from the way he looked at her.'

Lambert stood by the window drinking his coffee, looking out at the back yard, transformed with coloured paving slabs and a roofed-in area for sitting out, bright with tubs of forsythia and flowering currant. A white plaster figure of a cupid held aloft an urn planted with trailing variegated ivy. 'I never go into the shop now,' Mrs Snape said. 'Not after the way Arnold behaved towards me after his Dad died.'

She took the lettuce over to the sink and began to wash it. 'He could hardly wait till his Dad was cold before he told me I wouldn't be wanted any more.' She gave a resentful jerk of her head. 'He didn't mince his words either. He more or less implied I'd been leading the life of Riley for the last few years, a nice cushy job, getting paid for doing damn-all.'

She shook the lettuce vigorously in a wire basket; drops of water flew about the kitchen. 'I didn't demean myself by arguing with him. I just gathered up my bits and pieces and walked out. I've never set foot inside the place from that day to this.' She glanced at Lambert. 'I had no quarrel with the girls. I always spoke to them if I saw them in the street, but that was as far as it went.'

She arranged the lettuce in a glass bowl and began to slice

tomatoes and cucumber. 'It's certainly no hardship not to buy my meat there any more. I can buy it cheaper and better trimmed at any of the supermarkets in town. The business has gone right down since old Lockyear died. He had some first-class contracts with local hotels and restaurants, one or two school kitchens. He had a man with a van delivering full-time, used to go out round the local villages three times a week. All that's finished now, it's just Arnold and an apprentice lad.'

She cracked the shells of the hard-boiled eggs and stripped them swiftly and cleanly, sliced them neatly on a little aluminium gadget. 'No, Arnold isn't the butcher his father was, nor the businessman. He hasn't the manner either, he never has two words to say, not in the way of friendly chat while he's serving you. He's downright surly sometimes.' She disposed the egg slices in an artistic pattern over the salad. 'I don't know if he'll have the face to open the shop tomorrow, but if he does there won't be many from round here that'll go in. By next weekend he'll be standing behind his counter twiddling his thumbs.'

She set about opening the various tins. 'He never got on with those two poor girls. He never liked them, he was always jealous of them. He couldn't see why he should have to be responsible for them after his father died. He always wanted them to clear off out of the way, and the sooner the better. He kept his mouth shut while his father was alive, of course, but I could see well enough what was going on inside his head. It didn't take a mind-reader to do that.'

She took a tin of little homemade cakes from a shelf and set them out on a platter, handing Lambert a couple as an afterthought. 'Arnold drove those two girls out of the house—or as good as, whatever he likes to tell you now.'

'Would you have expected Joanne to phone him while she was away?' Lambert asked. 'To let him know how she was getting on?'

She shook her head at once, with decision. 'No, not her.

The less he knew about anything they were doing, the better those girls were pleased, that was always the way it was.' She gave him a shrewd glance. 'I'll tell you something, though: the last thing in the world Arnold would have wanted would be for Joanne to find Helen and talk her into coming back home.'

'Have you spoken to Arnold since all this came out?'

'No, I have not, nor intend to.'

'Have any of the neighbours been to see him?'

'Not they. What could they say to him?'

'Has he any relatives round here?'

'Not that I ever heard of.'

'Is he in the house now?'

'I expect so, I haven't seen him go out. And in any case, where would he go? He's never been one for the pub.' She paused. 'I suppose he could be down at his allotment, but I doubt it. He wouldn't want the other men watching him, talking behind his back.' She glanced up at the clock and uttered a sharp exclamation.

'I'll get along out of your way,' Lambert said. 'You don't happen to know of any special friends either of the girls may have had locally?'

'They certainly neither of them ever had any boyfriends,' she said at once. 'Arnold would never have allowed them to bring a boy home. Not that either of them was ever interested in boys, from anything I could see.' She flashed him an upward glance. 'More interested in getting away from here altogether, putting some distance between themselves and their precious stepbrother.' She pondered. 'I can't remember any special friend of Helen's, but there was a girl Joanne used to pal about with. Michelle Kershaw, number eleven Chadcote Road. It isn't five minutes' walk from here.'

She came to the door and gave him directions. Lambert could see the curtains move at the windows of more than one house in the terrace opposite. He turned his head and glanced at the butcher's shop next door. He had a vision of

Lockyear inside, alone, sitting in silence in the kitchen or lying upstairs on his bed, staring up at the ceiling.

Mrs Snape followed his glance. 'He's got what he wanted now all right,' she said with an edge of malice. 'He's got the whole place to himself at last. I only hope he's satisfied.'

The houses that faced each other across Chadcote Road were smaller and older than those in Thirlstane Street, the brickwork crumbling, the paintwork faded, a general air of seediness.

Lambert's ring at the door of No. 11 was answered after a minute or two by a flustered-looking, middle-aged woman. 'What is it?' she demanded, already half turned away again, back to whatever she had been snatched from.

Lambert disclosed his identity and the nature of his inquiry. Conflicting expressions flitted across her face. She was clearly torn between a strong desire to pump him for every drop of information and the equally powerful necessity to return to what she had been doing.

'You'd better come in,' she flung at him half angrily after a few moments. He stepped inside and she banged the door shut. The house smelled of perfumed bath salts—expensive French bath salts, if Lambert's nose was any judge.

'I warn you,' Mrs Kershaw added, 'Michelle can't stop long gabbing, she's on her way out. She's got this young man calling for her at half past, he's taking her home to supper. It's the first time he's asked her, she's only known him a few weeks.' She looked earnestly up at him in the narrow hall. 'He lives out on Jubilee Drive'—as if the name must strike awed respect into all who heard it. She saw that it meant nothing to him. 'Those lovely new houses,' she added. She made a gesture indicating expansiveness, conditions very different from Chadcote Road. 'She can't keep his parents waiting, they must see she knows what's what.'

A door opened along the hall and a girl's head appeared, covered in blue plastic rollers swathed in a film of white chiffon. She looked very like what her mother must have been twenty-five years ago; her frowning expression showed what she would look like herself in another quarter of a century. 'It's nearly twenty to,' she said to her mother loudly, with accusation. She barely glanced at Lambert.

'It's this gentleman,' her mother told her, in a tone now markedly placatory. 'He's from the police. Come to ask some questions about Joanne Mowbray.'

'I didn't know her all that well,' Michelle said at once. She came out into the hall. She wore a nylon petticoat richly flounced with lace; her bare legs were thrust into fluffy mules. She had a tiny waist, a beautiful bosom, neat and rounded. Lambert strove to raise his eyes to the level of her glowering countenance.

'I won't keep you long,' he promised.

'You'd better come on in.' Mrs Kershaw led the way along the hall. 'I can finish your dress while we talk,' she added to Michelle. Lambert followed them into a small, crowded living-room. A table in the centre of the room held a sewing-machine. Mrs Kershaw picked up a sleeveless dress of beautiful flowered silk and slipped it over Michelle's head. She knelt down and began to pin up the hem. 'Don't make it too long,' Michelle warned.

'I understand you were a friend of Joanne's,' Lambert said.

Michelle pulled down the corners of her mouth. Before she could speak her mother put in, 'They were never really friends, and she hardly knew Helen at all. She never went to the house, not in recent years.'

'Joanne sat next to me at school,' Michelle told him. 'We used to walk home together. That was all.'

'They never went out together,' Mrs Kershaw added. 'No one could say they were at all close.'

Michelle turned to let her mother deal with the back of the dress. 'Joanne never went anywhere. Not after her stepfather died. Her stepbrother never gave her any pocket money.

When she was turned thirteen she got herself a Saturday job, at a greengrocer's. After that she always had a little job somewhere or other, but she never spent any of the money, she used to pay it straight into the post office. She never went on holiday, or on any of the school trips, not after Mr Lookyear died.'

'Did she have any boyfriends?'

She shook her head. 'She didn't have any time for boy-friends.'

'Did she tell you she was going to Cannonbridge?'

'No, I didn't know anything about that. I'd hardly seen her since we left school.' She revolved again.

'Michelle's at the College of Further Education,' her mother told Lambert with pride and satisfaction. 'She's taking a commercial course, she's doing very well.'

'Was it you that saw Helen Mowbray coming out of a café in Cannonbridge about three years ago?' Lambert asked Michelle. 'And told Joanne about it?'

A glance flashed between mother and daughter.

'No, it wasn't me,' Michelle said blandly. 'I don't know anything about that.'

Mrs Kershaw added the final pin and sat back on her heels. 'There you are,' she told Michelle. 'Run up and take a look in the mirror.'

Michelle ran out of the room and up the stairs. 'What a terrible business about the Mowbray girls,' Mrs Kershaw said to Lambert. 'I don't want Michelle mixed up in any of it. A girl with her looks, at her age, she could go anywhere, marry anyone. You can't be too careful, people soon get the wrong idea.'

CHAPTER 5

Late on Monday evening it began to rain, by midnight it was raining heavily. The downpour continued through the night. Much more of this and we'll have the river over its banks, Sergeant Lambert thought as he drove to work on Tuesday morning. The private sector of industry and commerce would resume work today after the Easter break; the public sector would, in its customary fashion, allow itself another day or two of leisure.

Information continued to flow in, all of it to be painstakingly sifted, sorted, investigated.

A minute or two after nine o'clock Kelsey and Lambert hurried through the drenching rain up the steps of the Cannonbridge Secretarial Agency. This was a highly reputable concern, still with something of the flavour of the Victorian era in which it had been founded. It occupied the ground floor of a fine old building not far from the town centre.

The Principal, Miss Bosworth, was expecting them. She had phoned on Monday to say that she had had some acquaintance with both the Mowbray girls. She was a tall, thin lady of uncertain age with a high forehead, scanty hair drawn back into a bun; she wore a severely tailored dark grey suit and a white blouse fastened at the neck with a cameo brooch. Apart from the length of her skirt, it seemed to Sergeant Lambert that she could have sat behind her desk on the day the agency opened its doors, without looking in any way out of place.

Her manner was distant but civil. She displayed no curiosity about the case but appeared concerned merely with performing her duty as a citizen, supplying what assistance she could in order to be done with the whole distasteful business as speedily as possible.

Helen Mowbray had first called at the agency four years ago. She had excellent qualifications, first-class references, was intelligent and well-mannered, self-possessed and articulate. She had struck Miss Bosworth as more than ordinarily ambitious, keen to work hard and get on; Miss Bosworth had been happy to take her on to the books.

Helen had been sent out on a number of local jobs; Miss Bosworth supplied a list of these postings. 'After she had been with us a few months,' she told Kelsey, 'we sent her to Wyatt Fashions as a holiday relief. At the end of her stint they offered her a permanent post, which she accepted.' She moved a hand. 'That's a common occurrence in this business. But she didn't settle at Wyatt's. She stayed there three or four months, then she set up on her own, freelancing. I think it was mainly a matter of temperament, she preferred to feel in control of her life, that if she worked hard she would get all the rewards herself. She called in here from time to time if she wasn't very busy, she did occasional work for us. And I phoned her sometimes if we were particularly pressed, to ask if she could fit in a special job. If she could manage it, she always obliged us. She was a businesslike girl, methodical and professional in all she did.'

She sat back in her chair. 'Then she was offered another permanent post, and again she accepted it. It was at Fletcher's Plastics. They offered her a good salary and the offer came at a time when things were a little slack for her.' Miss Bosworth had had no further contact with Helen after she went to Fletcher's.

'Did you know anything about her personal life?' Kelsey asked. 'Any men friends?'

She shook her head. 'She wasn't given to discussing her personal affairs. Or to sit about chattering during business hours.' She gave a prim little smile. 'Neither am I.'

'Would you have thought her a girl to provoke a violent reaction?'

She looked at him thoughtfully. 'I imagine she was capable of being ruthless. She was certainly single-minded.'

Joanne Mowbray had called at the agency on the morning of Monday, February 28th, as soon as the doors opened. Miss Bosworth had told her what she knew. 'She was nowhere near as good-looking as Helen,' she said, 'but you couldn't mistake them for sisters. The same build and colouring.' She tilted back her head. 'And you had the same impression with them both, that they'd hang on like bull terriers if they got their teeth into something. Or someone.'

The firm of builders who had demolished Holmwood, the house on the Tappenhall Road, in order to erect a block of old people's flats, readily supplied the name of the person from whom they had bought the dwelling: a Mr Vincent Udell, a small-scale property developer with an address in a residential suburb of Cannonbridge.

Towards the end of Tuesday morning Sergeant Lambert drove Kelsey over there, but there was no one at home. As they came out of the gate again an elderly woman came towards them, huddled under an umbrella. She paused to tell them, 'If you're looking for the Udells, they're not at home, they went away for Easter.'

'Do you know when they'll be back?' Kelsey asked.

'I should think it would be some time this evening. Wednesday is one of Mrs Udell's mornings at the Almost New boutique.' This was a charity shop in the town. 'She wouldn't miss her turn there, she's very conscientious.'

'We'll go along to Wyatt Fashions,' Kelsey said as they got back into the car. There had been a phone call from Wyatt's earlier in the morning to say that the firm had some knowledge of both Mowbray girls. Lambert turned the car back towards the centre of town.

The main branch of Wyatt's occupied a prime position in a handsome Regency promenade in the main shopping area. A double-fronted emporium—shop was too undistinguished an appellation for so upmarket an enterprise—a good deal of greenery and floral decoration about the entrance and windows; lengths of crushed velvet in subtle hues, artfully arranged; some graceful, unusual ferns in ornate Victorian plant pots—but no sign from the outside of anything as brashly obvious as a garment. Only the curly, flowing gilt lettering over the entrance: Wyatt Fashions, gave any clue to the nature of the establishment.

The reception area provided a few more clues: a bridal creation in silk and ruffled lace in delicate shades of ivory; a little further on, an elegant outfit of hat, dress and jacket—for the bride's mother, Lambert was deciding, when a very superior-looking young woman approached them.

The Chief disclosed their identities and asked if he could have a word with the owner of the business, Mrs Julia Wyatt. The girl took herself off and the two men stood glancing about as they waited. Neither of them had ever set foot inside the premises before, though Lambert had often glanced at the foliage and fabrics as he walked past.

Kelsey had made inquiries about the firm before setting out this morning. It seemed that the business had been founded some fifty years ago by Mrs Wyatt's late husband. Shortly after the death of his first wife he had married Julia, at that time employed by the firm as a model; she was thirty-five years his junior. There were no children of either marriage and when Wyatt died nine years later he left everything to Julia. In the twelve years the business had been under her direction it had steadily progressed. There were now half a dozen subsidiary branches scattered across the county, with plans for still further expansion. The factory—much enlarged since Wyatt's death—was situated near a small town twelve miles to the south-west of Cannonbridge.

The young woman returned to say that Mrs Wyatt would see them. She led the way along a thickly carpeted corridor, past showrooms where Lambert caught dazzling glimpses of evening wear, day wear, sports wear. She opened a door into an area where the glamour temperature took a sudden sharp dive. Uncarpeted floors, offices and workrooms decorated in a sober, businesslike fashion, an atmosphere of uncompromising efficiency.

Mrs Wyatt was seated behind a large desk in her office. She stood up to greet them. A tall, well-built woman of formidable presence; she had clearly once been a beauty and was still striking-looking. Nothing that money, time or effort could do to seal off her looks from the erosions of the advancing years had apparently been spared—but there's a limit to what even those powerful weapons can do, Sergeant Lambert thought as Kelsey spoke to her.

Mrs Wyatt had learned of the discovery of the two bodies when she came into the building this morning. She had been away over the Easter weekend, had got back last night. Her secretary had spoken to her of the matter, had told her that Helen Mowbray had worked for the firm for a brief spell a few years ago. Mrs Wyatt wouldn't have been aware of that herself, the recruitment of office staff was the responsibility of the office supervisor. She very much doubted that she had ever seen or spoken to Helen; the girl had worked in the general office. She hadn't been dismissed; it seemed she had decided to leave and try her luck at freelance work. She had worked satisfactorily while she was with them and they had given her a good reference; the firm had had no further contact with her after she left.

Kelsey asked her if Joanne Mowbray had called at Wyatt's, inquiring about her sister. 'I understand that she did,' Mrs Wyatt told him. 'Of course I knew nothing about it at the time. I heard about it this morning. I gather she spoke to the office supervisor.'

'We'd better have a word with her,' Kelsey said.

'Yes, of course.' Mrs Wyatt spoke to her secretary and a few minutes later the supervisor came into the room. Fifty or so, she looked able and intelligent; she seemed on good terms with Mrs Wyatt.

Yes, she remembered Helen Mowbray. Kelsey asked if she could recall anything during Helen's time with the firm that might have any bearing on the case. She shook her head. Helen's stay had been entirely unremarkable; there had been no disagreements with any of the staff. She had made no special friend while she was there. 'She was a quiet girl,' the supervisor added. 'She kept very much to herself. It wasn't that she was unfriendly, she was always well-mannered. She just didn't join in, but it didn't give offence.'

Joanne Mowbray had called at Wyatt's during the afternoon of Tuesday, March 1st. The supervisor had spoken to her, had told her what little she knew.

'You didn't mention the matter to Mrs Wyatt?'

'No.'

'Why not?'

She looked surprised. 'It didn't occur to me to tell her, I didn't attach much importance to it. I have full responsibility for the office, I'm accustomed to dealing with anything that arises myself.' She never once glanced at Mrs Wyatt as she answered his questions but he had a strong feeling of close understanding between the two women, a sense of their standing shoulder to shoulder against the outsider.

When they left they weren't taken back through the hallowed front area but conducted discreetly to a rear exit which brought them out into a narrow rain-soaked alley overlooked by the homely backs of the stately buildings on the promenade.

Kelsey frowned as they walked back to the car. 'What did you make of that?' he asked Lambert.

'Seemed straightforward enough. I should think Madam Wyatt runs a pretty tight ship. Not a lady I should care to tangle with.'

'You didn't get the impression there was something they weren't mentioning?'

'No, I can't say I did. I certainly got the impression they weren't best pleased to have policemen tramping over their carpets. Can't really blame them, they'd hardly want to advertise that one of the Mowbray girls had worked there. Brutal murders wouldn't mix very well with their glossy image.'

Kelsey gave a grunt. 'You may be right.' He looked at his watch. 'We'll get back to the station, see what's doing, have a bite to eat. Then we'll go along to Fletcher's.' A far more down-to-earth enterprise, Fletcher's, manufacturers and suppliers of plastic goods to the building trade—but possibly no more anxious than Wyatt's to establish in the public mind any connection, however remote or tenuous, with the discovery of the horrifying remains of a beautiful girl in a dilapidated privy beside a decaying dwelling in a distant field.

An hour later when the Chief was coming up from the canteen there was a message from the desk: someone on the phone about the Mowbray case, wanting to speak to him. He made the last flight of steps in good time but the desk sergeant had already replaced the receiver by the time Kelsey reached him.

'Sorry, Chief,' the sergeant said. 'Couldn't persuade her to hang on. A young woman, by the sound of her. She wouldn't give her name or address, she just said she works at Wyatt Fashions.'

'I knew it!' Kelsey struck the air with his fist.

The sergeant glanced down at the notes he had scribbled. 'She said: Go and talk to David Hinckley, ask him what he knows about Helen Mowbray. She said he's one of Wyatt's designers, he lives out at Grayshott Manor, Mrs Wyatt's place. You can catch him on his own most mornings, he has a studio there.'

The rain was beginning to slacken as they left Cannonbridge; by the time they reached Grayshott Manor it had ceased. The manor was a fine seventeenth-century dwelling standing in beautiful wooded countryside, some eight miles to the west of Cannonbridge.

They were admitted by the housekeeper, a woman in late middle age with a competent air and pleasant manner. Kelsey told her his name, but not his profession or the nature of his business.

Yes, Mr Hinckley was in his studio, she would find out if he could see them. She left them in the oak-panelled hall and went off towards the rear of the house. She returned a few minutes later to say that Mr Hinckley would be along shortly. She showed them into a sitting-room, exquisitely furnished and meticulously cared for.

When she had gone Kelsey prowled about the room, examining and peering. He stood back to stare up at an oil painting to one side of the fireplace. It showed an elderly man with a narrow, unsmiling face, a deeply lined forehead, a long upper lip and stubborn chin.

'The late Mr Wyatt, I take it,' Kelsey said. Whatever she'd married him for, it wouldn't appear to have been for his fatal beauty.

The door opened and a young man came into the room. Twenty-six or seven, tall, with a supple, loose-limbed build. He was exceptionally good-looking but with nothing showy about his appearances; dark blonde hair, eyes of brilliant blue. No wonder la Wyatt keeps him shut away out here, Lambert thought, safely distanced from the ravening female employees.

Kelsey disclosed their identities and the nature of their inquiries. Hinckley showed no surprise—but then, Kelsey reflected, Mrs Wyatt might have lunched at the Manor, or at least spoken to him over the phone since their visit to Wyatt Fashions.

Hinckley took his seat in an armchair, facing them. He leaned back in a relaxed attitude, his face wore an easy, casual look. But underneath he's tense and edgy, Lambert thought. Hinckley's eyes suddenly began a rapid blinking and after a moment he put up a hand and leaned his forehead against it, resting his elbow on the arm of his chair, shading his traitorous eyes with his fingers.

'You live here at the Manor?' Kelsey asked. Hinckley gave a nod.

'How long have you lived here?'

'Two or three years.'

'I should like an answer a good deal more precise than that,' Kelsey said crisply.

'I can't give you the exact date offhand,' Hinckley answered in an easy, pleasant tone. 'I should have to look it up.'

'Then look it up,' Kelsey told him. 'We can wait.'

Hinckley got to his feet and stood irresolute, then he said, 'I remember now. I moved in here two years ago last December, at the beginning of December.' He sat down again, no longer leaning back but upright and alert.

'And before you moved in here,' Kelsey said, 'I take it you had been for some time on intimate terms with Mrs Wyatt?'

Hinckley gave the Chief a long, wary look, then he nodded.

'I also take it,' Kelsey said, 'that during the time Helen Mowbray worked for Wyatt Fashions, you formed an association with her?'

Hinckley stared at the Chief like a mesmerized rabbit, then he turned his head and looked down at the floor.

'Mrs Wyatt became aware of the association,' the Chief went on as if Hinckley had answered and the answer had been Yes. 'She didn't relish the notion so she gave Helen her marching orders.'

Hinckley glanced up at the Chief. 'Julia—Mrs Wyatt—didn't sack her,' he said on a defensive note. 'They had a talk and afterwards Helen gave in her notice. Julia gave her a good reference.'

'Did Mrs Wyatt discuss the matter with you at the time?'

Hinckley nodded. I doubt if discuss is an exact description of what took place, Sergeant Lambert thought.

'Did Mrs Wyatt tell you what she proposed to do about Helen?'

Again Hinckley nodded.

'Did you raise any objection?'

Hinckley shook his head.

'Did you continue your association with Helen after she left Wyatt's?'

'No, I did not.' He held himself very still, his eyes recommenced their rapid blink.

'You're certain of that?'

'Yes, I am.'

'You never laid eyes on Helen again?'

He moved a hand. 'I saw her once or twice, just by chance. I didn't stop to speak to her.'

'Why not?'

Hinckley moved his shoulders but made no reply.

'Did you have dealings of any kind with Helen after she left Wyatt's?' Kelsey pressed him. He shook his head. 'Contact of any kind at all?' Kelsey persisted. Again he shook his head.

'How did she take it when she had to leave Wyatt's?'

'She understood, she knew how things were, she'd known that all along. She didn't really mind. We'd only known each other a short time—and in any case she'd been thinking of setting up in business on her own.'

'What were your feelings when you heard about the discovery of her body?'

A flicker of anger showed on Hinckley's face. 'Naturally I was upset,' he answered in a controlled voice.

'Very upset?'

Hinckley stared back at him. 'Enough.'

'Was Mrs Wyatt upset?'

'I couldn't say.'

'Did you discuss it with her?' Hinckley shook his head.

'Neither of you referred to the matter?' Again he shook his head.

'Why was that?' Kelsey persisted. 'A girl you had both

known, a discovery that set every tongue in the locality wagging—but neither of you so much as spoke her name.'

The muscles tightened along Hinckley's jaw. 'You know perfectly well why not,' he said abruptly.

'No, I can't say that I do know,' Kelsey observed. 'I could think of half a dozen different explanations but I've no idea if any of them is the right one. Perhaps you'd enlighten me.'

Hinckley exhaled a long breath. 'Julia is a jealous woman,' he said flatly. 'There would have been no point in stirring all that up again.'

'Stirring all what up?' Kelsey echoed sharply.

'All that was said between Julia and me three and a half years ago when she got rid of—when Helen left Wyatt's.'

'And precisely what was said between you three and a half years ago?'

Hinckley frowned. 'The usual sort of thing.' He made a gesture of irritation. 'Accusations, charges. You must surely know the kind of thing when a woman is jealous.' I very much doubt the Chief's had Hinckley's range of experience on that subject, Sergeant Lambert thought.

'What was the extent of your association with Helen Mowbray?' Kelsey asked.

'I took her out a few times, to a meal, or a cinema.'

'Did you go to bed with her?' Hinckley shook his head.

'It seems a slender foundation for Mrs Wyatt's jealousy.'

'A jealous woman doesn't need a strong foundation,' Hinckley said with feeling.

'Did Joanne Mowbray make any kind of contact with you?' Hinckley shook his head. 'Did you know she called at Wyatt's to inquire about Helen?'

Hinckley shifted in his chair. 'No, I didn't.'

'When did you hear that she had called there?'

Hinckley looked very uneasy. 'I didn't know until this moment.'

'You're sure of that?'

'Yes.'

Kelsey gave him a long hard stare. 'How long have you worked for Wyatt's?' he asked abruptly.

Hinckley seemed relieved at the sudden switch, his manner relaxed fractionally. 'Four years,' he answered. 'Almost five now. Ever since I left art college.'

'Where were you living before you moved in here?'

'In a flat in Cannonbridge.'

'If we could have the address,' Kelsey said. Hinckley gave it to him.

'What position do you hold with Wyatt's?'

'I'm a senior designer.'

'Is all your work done here?'

'No. I do my own designing here and I also deal with the buying in of some outside designs. I go over to the factory most afternoons.'

'How long have you held the post?'

'About two and a half years.'

'You were appointed at the same time as you moved into Grayshott Manor?' He gave a nod. 'What was your previous position in the firm?'

'I worked down at the Cannonbridge branch.'

'In what capacity?'

'As personal assistant to Mrs Wyatt.'

'Were you originally engaged in that capacity?'

'No. I was taken on in the design room.'

'I imagine there was a substantial increase in salary when you were appointed to your present post?' Hinckley nodded. 'And plenty of perks? Free board and lodging? A car? Holidays? Free use of phone?' He's trying to make him lose his temper, Lambert thought. But Hinckley sat silent and unmoving, his face blank and disciplined. Two years of living with Madam Julia would probably teach him how to control his temper, Lambert thought, if he didn't know how to control it before.

Kelsey pushed back his chair and stood up to leave. In the doorway he paused and looked back at Hinckley who still sat in his chair. 'And the last time you saw Helen Mowbray?' Kelsey asked.

Hinckley flashed him a glance. 'I told you—I saw her once or twice after she left Wyatt's but I didn't speak to her.'

'You would swear to that in court?'

'Yes, I would.'

At the sound of the sitting-room door opening the house-keeper came out from the kitchen quarters to conduct them to the front door. On the threshold Kelsey turned and asked her, 'Did you have any acquaintance with either of the Mowbray girls?'

She looked startled. 'You mean those two poor girls?' Kelsey nodded. 'No, of course not,' she answered with force. 'How ever would I know them?'

'Did you ever see either of them here?'

'No, of course not.' She seemed astounded. 'What would they be doing here?'

'Did Joanne Mowbray call or phone here, asking for Mr Hinckley?' Kelsey persisted.

She shook her head with energy. Kelsey said no more but went off to the car. She remained in the doorway, staring after them in frowning puzzlement as the car moved off down the drive.

CHAPTER 6

The firm of J. Preston Fletcher was a flourishing business, comprising half a dozen concerns, all situated within twenty miles of Cannonbridge, each dealing with a different aspect of the building trade. Fletcher lived a little way out of Cannonbridge and much of the group work was handled from his office at the plastics factory on the industrial estate.

There had been a phone call during the morning from Fletcher's secretary to say that the firm had had some dealings with the Mowbray girls. It was late in the afternoon when Sergeant Lambert drove into the car park.

Neither Kelsey nor Lambert had met Fletcher although his face had become familiar to them in recent weeks from posters, leaflets, photographs in the local paper—Fletcher was putting up for the council in May and was conducting a shrewd and energetic campaign. He was said to have an eye on Westminster and there were those who didn't doubt he'd get there before many years had gone by.

Fletcher's secretary, Mrs Ogilvie, an intelligent-looking woman in her thirties with a quietly efficient manner, was busy at her desk. Yes, Mr Fletcher was here, not actually in the office, he was over in the stockroom with a customer. 'I can get him for you if you insist,' she told Kelsey, 'but I'd rather not interrupt unless it's absolutely essential.' She made a little face. 'There's a big order on the cards. I wouldn't want to disturb them at a tricky moment. I know Mr Fletcher won't be more than another five or ten minutes, the customer has a plane to catch.'

Kelsey didn't mind waiting. He asked if she had known Helen Mowbray but she told him no, she hadn't worked at Fletcher's in Helen's day. She had spoken to Joanne Mowbray, once in person and once over the phone. Joanne had called at the office during the afternoon of Monday, February 28th, inquiring about her sister. Mrs Ogilvie told her she had no personal knowledge of Helen; she had called Mr Ryland in to speak to Joanne. Ryland was Fletcher's general assistant, responsible for the recruitment and management of office staff. He had spoken to Joanne in Mrs Ogilvie's presence, he had been unable to throw any light on Helen's whereabouts. He told Joanne he would make inquiries among the workforce and would mention the matter to Mr Fletcher who was over at one of his other factories that afternoon. Joanne said she would phone in a day or two to see if he'd had any success.

'She rang a couple of days later, on the Wednesday

afternoon,' Mrs Ogilvie told the Chief. About three o'clock, to the best of her recollection. She had answered the phone herself. Mr Ryland was out at the time; Mr Fletcher was very busy but he had spoken to Joanne. She didn't know what was said, she had had to go over to the annexe for some files and when she got back a customer came in; she'd forgotten about Joanne's call. Later in the afternoon when she remembered it she asked Mr Fletcher if Joanne was having any luck with her inquiries. He said she'd had no positive leads but was still hopeful. He'd told Joanne they hadn't discovered any further information themselves. Joanne had given him her home address in Martleigh, in case they learned of anything later.

A man came across the yard and into the office. Not much above middle height, with a strong-looking, muscular frame; dark hair, dark eyes, a deeply tanned skin. Around forty, Kelsey judged. An alert, on-the-ball look—and a look too of a man who might be prepared to give an account of himself with his fists, and might have had experience along those lines; his nose looked as if it had been broken and reset. 'My name's Ryland, Jack Ryland,' he told the Chief. 'I heard you were here.'

Yes, he had known Helen Mowbray. 'She came here as a holiday relief,' he said. 'She was very efficient. I suggested she might like a permanent job.' He moved his shoulders. 'But she didn't settle. I wasn't really surprised, she was an independent type. She stayed three or four months, then she went back to freelancing.'

He had looked up the date on which she had left the firm: March 26th, three years ago. Fletcher's had had no further dealings with her and Ryland had never come across her again.

'What work did she do while she was here?' Kelsey asked.

'She worked in the general office.' He took them along a corridor into a room where five clerks were seated at desks: three girls, a youngish married woman, and an older, grey-haired spinster. One of the girls was rather pretty, Lambert saw, with a head of gold-auburn hair, thick and shining. Her eyes went at once to Ryland; he flicked her a glance Lambert couldn't read.

Ryland introduced the two men and Kelsey asked if any of the clerks had known Helen Mowbray. The three girls shook their heads. The married woman said she had been there in Helen's day but had scarcely known her. 'She was very reserved,' she said. Helen had got on with her work, had scarcely ever joined in general conversation. The woman had seen her once or twice in Cannonbridge after she left but they hadn't spoken.

The older woman had also known Helen to the same minimal extent. Kelsey asked her if Helen had had any association with any of the male workers. She looked at him in surprise. 'She wasn't the type to go into the works, or stand about chatting to the men,' she said with certainty. The younger woman nodded in agreement.

After they left the office Kelsey went along with Ryland into the works. Ryland had a word with the foreman and then spoke to the men over the loudspeaker, introducing Kelsey. The Chief asked anyone who might be able to shed any light on the murders either to come forward to speak to him now or to call in at the main police station without delay.

There was no immediate response and Ryland took them back to the office, where Mrs Ogilvie had provided coffee. As they were drinking it Preston Fletcher came in. He apologized for keeping them waiting. 'We got a very good order,' he said with a smile. He shook hands with the two policemen. He was a big, athletically built man with a strong physical presence. An open, amiable face, light brown hair and light brown eyes, a bracing manner, energetic and cordial. He exuded an air of confidence and optimism that Sergeant Lambert had noticed before in self-made men who had done well by a comparatively early age; he judged Fletcher to be thirty-five or -six.

'This is an appalling business,' Fletcher said. 'I dare say

Mrs Ogilvie has put you in the picture, told you what we know about the two girls. I'm afraid it's not a great deal. Mrs Ogilvie phoned me on Monday evening to tell me about it—my wife and I had been at the cottage over Easter. I've thought about it a lot since then but I'm afraid I haven't been able to come up with anything useful. I didn't have anything to do with Helen myself, the office staff is the province of my good friend here.' He nodded at Ryland.

Kelsey asked if he could recall exactly what Joanne had said during her phone call on the Wednesday afternoon.

'We didn't talk for long,' Fletcher told him. 'I was pretty busy at the time and I didn't really have anything to tell her. I was sorry for the girl, she seemed a decent type, she wanted to put the money to good use. She said she was giving up and going back home that evening. I suggested she might try putting ads in various papers and she said she'd already decided to do that, it was the only other thing she could think of.'

'You're certain she told you she'd decided to go home that evening?' Kelsey pressed him. 'She didn't just say she was thinking about it?'

Fletcher pondered. 'Now you query it,' he said after some moments, 'I'm afraid I can't be absolutely certain.' He pondered again, frowning, then he shook his head. 'No, I'm sorry, I can't be sure either way.'

The Almost New boutique stood at the end of a terrace of small shops in an outlying area of Cannonbridge. On Wednesday morning Lambert parked the car in a side street and he and Kelsey walked round to the boutique.

The windows were full of astonishing bargains, men's shirts for a pound, sports jackets for a fiver. Inside Kelsey could see rails of garments, a row of curtained cubicles. Two middle-aged women stood behind a large table, facing a young man who had just placed before them a suitcase secured with leather straps. As he unbuckled the straps the women looked on, pleased and stimulated, like terriers scenting a rat. A dozen or so folk, mostly women, wandered among the stands, fingering, examining. One of the women came into view round the end of a rail, with a young lad beside her; they scrutinized the garments with concentrated attention. 'That's Mrs Cooney,' Lambert said to Kelsey. 'And Graham. From the Parkfield estate.' Kelsey gave them an abstracted glance. He pushed open the door and went inside.

The interior was warm and stuffy with a musty overlay, stale perfume and old deodorant. Graham Cooney glanced round and his eyes met Lambert's. Lambert smiled and raised a hand in greeting. Graham gave him the barest nod in reply, he turned back to the rail and resumed his examination of the garments.

Lambert followed the Chief up to the table. The two women paid them no attention. They were now delving into the suitcase with rapid, eager movements, bringing out the treasures, exclaiming, assessing, in loud conversational tones; the young man stood silently by with an expressionless face.

'My first go, this time,' one of the women said with fierce determination. 'You had first go last time.' She held a blouse against herself. The other woman gave a resentful jerk of a nod.

'Is that all then?' the young man asked. 'All right if I push off?'

The first woman came out of her absorption with the blouse. 'Oh yes,' she said dismissingly. 'That's all right.' She returned her attention instantly to the blouse, frowning at the buttonholes, tugging at the seams. The young man turned and went out of the shop. The second woman took a sweater from the suitcase and examined the armpits with a detached, critical expression. Kelsey took a step nearer the table. She glanced up at him and said sharply, 'Men's clothing over there. Some perfectly good underwear for larger men on the fifty-pence rail—bereavement stuff, hardly worn.'

'I'm looking for a Mrs Udell,' Kelsey said. 'It's a business matter. I'd like a word with her.'

'She's back there.' The woman jerked her head towards a door at the end of the shop. 'I'll go and tell her,' she added reluctantly.

When she reached the door she turned her head and saw that the two men were following her. She flung Kelsey an authoritative look. 'Wait there,' she commanded. He came to a halt. She opened the door and went inside, closing the door firmly behind her. A minute or two later she came out again with another woman who looked questioningly at the Chief.

'Mrs Udell?' Kelsey asked. She gave a nod. The first woman went rapidly back to the suitcase.

Mrs Udell was a pleasant-looking woman with a thickening figure and greying hair, well groomed, well dressed in a comfortable matronly fashion. In a discreet tone Kelsey revealed his identity and asked if he might have a word with her. Alarm flashed across her face. 'It's nothing for you to worry about,' he assured her.

She led the way into the inner room which appeared to combine the functions of office, stockroom and kitchen.

'It's your husband I really want to see,' Kelsey told her. 'Perhaps you could tell us how we can get hold of him. We understand he used to own Holmwood, a house in Tappenhall Road. He rented a flat there at one time to Helen Mowbray.' He saw the name meant nothing to her. 'One of the two girls whose bodies were found—'

She uttered an exclamation and put a hand up to her face. She had heard of the double murder only half an hour ago when she came into the boutique; one of the other women had spoken of it but hadn't mentioned the girls' names.

'We'd like to speak to your husband,' Kelsey said. 'He may be able to give us valuable information.'

'Yes, of course,' she said at once. 'Vincent doesn't own any rented property these days, he sold it all off. He's working for Blackshaw now, Blackshaw's Construction, on the industrial estate.' Kelsey knew of the firm; it dealt mainly in extensions and loft conversions. 'But I'm afraid you won't find him over there now,' she added. 'He's out on calls all this morning, he handles that side of things, dealing with people who want a job done. But he'll be home for lunch.'

At twenty-five past one Sergeant Lambert turned the car into the road where the Udells lived. An estate car was parked outside the house; a fair-sized vehicle, light grey, four or five years old; it was immaculately clean, polished to a mirror-like gleam. Lambert slid the car in behind it. They got out and Kelsey stood looking at the estate car. He walked round it, peered inside. The rear seats were folded down and in the centre space were a couple of open cardboard boxes, one containing papers, leaflets, order books, the other holding samples, miniature windows, various types of cladding, all very neatly arranged.

Lambert's ring at the front door was answered by Mrs Udell. She took them into a kitchen where her husband sat at the table over his lunch. He made to get up but Kelsey waved him back into his chair.

Mrs Udell made the introductions. Udell was of average height and build; Kelsey put him in his early fifties. An everyday sort of face; sharp hazel eyes, bony features, thinning brown hair cut in a military fashion. Lambert noticed his ears, very small and pointed, with no lobes, set very close to his head. He was well groomed with a pink, clean-looking skin, well manicured hands, a gold signet ring set with a diamond on the little finger of his left hand. He was sprucely dressed in a dark business suit of expensive cut and first-class material; he wore a snowy shirt and had an equally snowy handkerchief, meticulously pointed, showing at his breast pocket.

'Sorry to trouble you while you're at your meal,' Kelsey said.

'Oh, Vincent doesn't mind,' Mrs Udell put in. 'He's only too anxious to do anything he can to help.' She offered them coffee which Kelsey accepted. Udell returned his attention to his portion of rhubarb tart, plentifully dredged with sugar, richly laced with cream. He ate carefully and delicately, with neat, precise movements.

'Your wife will have told you why we want to see you,' Kelsey said. 'If you could tell us about your dealings with Helen Mowbray, how you met her, how long you knew her, when you last saw her, and so on. Don't worry about getting it all in order, just say it as it comes.'

Udell pushed his plate aside and dabbed fastidiously at his lips with a napkin. When he finally spoke it was with some deliberation. 'I met her through Blackshaw's,' he told the Chief. 'I had dealings with them on and off for years, when I was in property. I was complaining to Blackshaw—this would be about three and a half years ago, maybe a bit more—about the amount of time it took doing my accounts. He told me he'd got a very good girl doing his, he'd got her through the Tradesmen's Agency. I gave her a try and I was very satisfied. After that she did my books when I didn't have time to do them myself.'

'How did she come to rent a flat from you?' Kelsey asked.

'She knew the sort of work I did, developing property. She told me one day she was looking for a flat herself. She knew I owned Holmwood, that the basement flat was coming vacant. I'd bought the house about four years before, with two sitting tenants. The house was in a very run-down state, it would have cost a fortune to put right. The tenant in the basement flat died a few months after I bought the house and after that I rented the flat out on short agreements, fully furnished.

'Helen asked me if she could have the flat. I told her I didn't intend letting it again. The other two floors were let

unfurnished as a maisonette to an old man, a scholarly sort of
chap, used to be an antiquarian bookseller at the other side of
the county before he retired. He spent his time writing
articles for learned magazines, doing a bit of research,
history, records, all that kind of thing. He lived in the ground
floor and used the first floor for his writing, one room as a
study and the others full of books and papers.

'He was over eighty and his health wasn't good. He'd
started talking about going into a nursing home, so naturally
I didn't want to let the basement flat again if I was going to
have the other two floors empty; what I wanted was possession of the whole house. I explained all that to Helen but
she kept on about it. She said it might be months before
Minshull—that was the old man's name—finally decided to
leave. If I let her have the flat she'd get out the moment I told
her she'd have to go.' He pulled down the corners of his
mouth. 'In the end I gave in and let her have the flat on
that definite understanding. She moved in as soon as it
came vacant. That was three years ago, the beginning of
April.'

'How long was she in the flat?'

'Eight months. Minshull told me at the end of October
that he'd finally decided to call it a day and go into a home.
He was starting to have blackouts and that frightened him.
He gave me a month's notice. I told Helen she had a month
to find somewhere else. She didn't raise any objection, she
kept to her bargain. I asked her a couple of weeks later if
she'd got somewhere to go and she said she had. She left at
the end of November, a couple of days after Minshull.'

'Where had Minshull gone?'

Udell gave him the name of a nursing home in a village
some twelve miles away. 'I don't know if he's still there,' he
added. 'Or even if he's still alive.'

'Did Helen tell you where she intended going after leaving
the flat?'

'No, she didn't. I gathered—more from her manner than

from anything she said—that she was going to some boy-friend.'

'Did you know of any boyfriend?'

'I didn't know anything about her private life. It was none of my business.'

'Did you know of any friends—male or female?' Udell shook his head.

'Did she do accounts for you while she occupied the flat?'

'Yes, from time to time. If I had some work for her I'd give her a ring, make an appointment to call round with it. I'd pick it up again when it was ready.'

'Did she leave a forwarding address for mail when she left the flat?'

'No. I asked her about that, the last time I saw her. I'd gone round to pick up some work she'd done for me. She'd already settled up the rent with me, she always paid that in advance. Her electricity and gas were paid by meter but there'd be a phone bill coming in after she'd gone. She gave me some money for that, it was more than enough. I told her I wouldn't need all that—she'd shown me her last couple of bills. She just laughed and said she'd rather leave too much than not enough; if there was anything over I could give it to Oxfam. I asked her where I should send any letters that came for her. She said she wasn't expecting any mail but if anything did come I was to keep it, she'd call round here from time to time to see if there was anything. But she never did call, and there was never any mail.'

'How were you proposing to get in touch with her next time you wanted some work done?'

'She told me she wouldn't be doing any more work for me, she was giving up freelancing. That was one of the things that made me think she might be going to live with some boy-friend. And her manner, her look when she said that, she was half-smiling.'

'You weren't curious?'

'No. I'm not a curious type.' He looked stolidly back at the Chief.

'Did she leave any belongings behind?'

'No, she took everything. As I said, the flat was fully furnished, so it was just her clothes and personal things.'

'What happened to the furniture and the other contents of the flat?'

'I sold the lot to a dealer.' He mentioned the name of a local man who specialized in house clearances. 'He had everything out of there a couple of days after Helen left. Minshull's maisonette was already empty.'

'Did you have any kind of contact with Helen after she left?'

'No, none at all.'

Kelsey asked Mrs Udell if she had ever met Helen Mowbray.

'Oh no,' she said with surprise. 'I wasn't married to Vincent then. We've only been married a couple of years.'

Kelsey heard the accents of the South Coast in her speech. 'You're not a local woman?' he said.

She smiled. 'No, I'm Dorset born and bred. Vincent came down for a summer holiday one year, I met him then. We were married a few months later, just before Christmas.' There was a brief silence. She seemed to feel something more was called for. 'I was a widow,' she added. 'I have a son by my first marriage. That's where we've been over Easter, staying with my son and his family down in Dorset.'

'And you?' Kelsey said to Udell. 'Are you a Cannonbridge man?'

'I've lived here a good many years,' Udell said. 'I look on myself as a Cannonbridge man by this time.'

'But you weren't born here?'

'He's from Tappenhall,' his wife said with an edge of raillery. Tappenhall was a small town twenty-five miles to the south. 'I've been living here more than two years now and I've never even set foot in Tappenhall. I asked Vincent to take me over there once or twice when we were first married.' She smiled. 'To revisit the haunts of his youth. But he point blank refused. He says it's a dead-and-alive hole, he was glad to get out of it, no one in his senses would ever go there voluntarily.' She laughed. 'I've given up asking him now.'

'I don't know that Tappenhall's as bad as all that,' Kelsey observed mildly.

Udell gave him a sardonic glance. 'Maybe you never had to live there.'

'But I did speak to Helen's sister,' Mrs Udell said. 'Joanne Mowbray.' Kelsey's head came sharply round. 'She phoned here one evening, on the Tuesday, that would be. I'd forgotten it, I remembered after you'd been into the boutique this morning. She asked if she could speak to my husband. I told her he was out. She explained what she wanted, about her sister and so on. She said she understood her sister had rented a flat from my husband. I didn't know anything about that of course, so I couldn't help her. I said she'd better ring again, later on that evening, when my husband would be in.'

'And did she ring again?'

'Yes. I asked Vincent about it after I got in—I had to go out that evening, it was my Needlework Guild. He said yes, she'd rung about eight o'clock.'

'I told Joanne more or less what I've just told you,' Udell said. 'That I didn't know where Helen had gone after she left the flat.'

'Did you hear from Joanne again?'

'No.'

'Would you be good enough to draw a map of Holmwood for us?' Kelsey asked him. 'The site, lay-out of the house, and so on. There's no need to go to a lot of trouble, all that's wanted is a simple straightforward plan, nothing fancy, just as long as it's clear.'

'Certainly, I'll do that,' Udell promised.

'Perhaps you could drop it in at the main police station. We'd like it as quickly as possible.'

'I'll do it this evening. I'll drop it in on my way to work in the morning.'

'That's very good of you,' Kelsey said. 'I gather you're not in property at all now?'

'No, I am not,' Udell said with feeling. 'I got fed up to the back teeth with it. Too much bureaucracy. Too many rights for the tenants and not enough for the landlord. It's got now so that it's a crime to own the roof over someone else's head. I decided to get out before they declared us all public enemies and strung us up from the nearest lamp-post.'

'When did you decide to pack it in?'

'A couple of years ago.'

'About the time you sold Holmwood?'

'Yes, around that time. I'm with Blackshaw now, I deal with the customer-relations side of the business, suits me very well. Blackshaw's very decent, very straightforward. He does first-class work, doesn't try to con the public, that's the way I like to do business.' He glanced at the clock. 'I have an appointment at two-forty-five.' He mentioned a village some miles away. 'I don't like to be late.'

Kelsey got to his feet. 'We'll let you get off, then. Good of you to spare us the time. We'll be looking in on Blackshaw when we leave here.'

'Joanne Mowbray phoned there as well,' Udell said. 'Blackshaw was telling me about it this morning. We'd decided to go along to the police station this evening, to tell you what we knew about the two girls. You'll find Blackshaw doesn't know any more than I've told you.'

'We'll have a word with him all the same,' Kelsey said. 'Got to go by the book in these matters.'

Blackshaw was a small, wiry man with a lively eye and a brisk manner; his business—half a mile or so from Fletcher's Plastics—appeared to be thriving and well run. Udell was

right, Blackshaw wasn't able to add anything of value to
what Udell had told them. Joanne had phoned Blackshaw on
the Wednesday morning; he had had no personal contact
with her, he had merely spoken to her over the phone. He had
told her that his last contact with Helen had been a couple of
months before she left Holmwood; he had no idea where she
might have gone after leaving the flat.

Kelsey asked him how he had spent the afternoon and
evening of that Wednesday, March 2nd. Blackshaw told him
they had been very busy just then, working overtime to
complete an important order. They had worked until eight
o'clock on the Wednesday as on the other evenings of that
week. He had got home dog-tired at about eight-thirty, had
eaten his supper, had slumped in front of the TV until
around ten, when he had gone to bed. His wife and schoolboy
son were both in the house all evening.

Kelsey looked at his watch as they left the industrial estate.
He had an appointment at three-thirty with the manager of
the bank where Helen Mowbray had had an account.

'Tomorrow,' he told Sergeant Lambert, 'after the inquest,
you'd better check Blackshaw's story. Then you can get over
to Tappenhall, see if you can come up with anything about
Vincent Udell. On the way back from Tappenhall you can
look in at that nursing home Udell mentioned, see if the old
man's still there, Minshull, see if he's got anything to say.'

CHAPTER 7

It rained steadily again throughout Wednesday night; the
downpour continued on Thursday morning. The double
inquest was set down for half past ten. The proceedings were
brief and formal, as was to be expected, the inquests being
merely opened and adjourned.

It was after half past eleven when Lambert set off for

Tappenhall; he had checked Blackshaw's story and it had stood up. The traffic was fairly heavy and it was the best part of an hour later that he reached the town centre. Tappenhall was a small, sleepy place; there was certainly no air of bustling prosperity. Workaday buildings, many with peeling paint and flaking stonework, looking more than usually disheartened in the drenching rain. Lambert parked his car and found a phone booth.

The directory revealed three entries under the name Udell with Tappenhall addresses: G. Udell; Mrs F. Udell; and W. L. Udell, Travel Agt., 56 Trinity Street. I'll try him first, Lambert decided. He left the booth and inquired for Trinity Street; it was by now twenty minutes to one.

He found the agency in a row of small dingy shops in a side street near the main shopping area. The window was full of brochures arranged without care for effect, the panes ornamented with stickers advertising cheap coach tours and cut-price holidays. Inside, a man sat behind the counter, gazing out at the rain with an air of habitual indifference, as if the last thing he expected was for the door to ping open to admit a customer.

Lambert pushed open the door and went in. The man gave him a routine look of mild inquiry and got slowly to his feet. Verging on fifty, Lambert judged—and clearly some relative of Vincent's Udell's. The same hazel eyes, though less sharp, and faintly bloodshot; the same bony features and thinning brown hair—badly in need of a trim.

Lambert revealed himself in the character of a citizen whose wife had suddenly wearied of the vagaries of the English spring and announced over breakfast that she wouldn't say no to an early holiday in some place where the sun could be guaranteed to shine. 'I'm in the town on business,' Lambert said. 'I happened to be passing and saw your stickers. I wondered if you'd got any bargains.'

Udell brought out brochures and directories. His movements released a waft of stale beer from his clothes. He answered Lambert's queries sensibly enough but asked scarcely any questions himself. After a few minutes he glanced up at the wall clock which showed four minutes to one.

'I close for lunch at one,' he stated on a take-it-or-leave-it note.

Lambert said as if on a sudden inspiration, 'I was thinking of going along to a pub for a sandwich. If you've nothing better to do, why don't you come along and bring the rest of the pamphlets?'

Some faint lightening appeared in Udell's expression. 'Right you are,' he said with the first trace of animation Lambert had seen. 'I won't be a jiffy.'

Five minutes later they were sitting in a nearby pub with pints of beer and plates of a very decent chicken pie in front of them. 'They pull a good pint here,' Udell said with deep appreciation. He took a long draught of his beer.

'Udell,' Lambert remarked idly. 'I came across a chap in Cannonbridge a few months ago with that name. He's in double glazing, porches and extensions, used to be in property at one time.'

'Vincent Udell?'

'Yes, I believe his name was Vincent.'

'Cousin of mine, first cousin. Is he a friend of yours?'

'No, I can't say he is. Casual acquaintance would be nearer the mark.'

Udell made a start on his chicken pie. 'I haven't heard of him for years. I knew he'd gone to Cannonbridge but I didn't know if he was still living there. Doing all right, is he? He used to pride himself on having a good head for business, always coming out on top.'

'He's doing well enough.'

'He's a year or two older than me,' Udell said. 'We lived in the same street when we were kids. He was an only child—his parents had been married I don't know how many years before he was born, they thought he was God's gift from heaven when he finally appeared.'

'He struck me as a bit of a dandy,' Lambert commented.

Udell laughed. 'He hasn't changed much, then. He always fancied himself, even as a kid. That was mainly his parents' doing. They had a very high opinion of themselves, pillars of the chapel, Sunday School teachers, all that sort of thing. They brought Vincent up to think he was a cut above the rest of us. They sent him to a private school, of course.'

His eyes sparkled with ancient spites and jealousies. 'Real little snob he was, never allowed to play with rough lads like me.' He gave a sardonic grin. 'Never allowed to go anywhere on his own, never allowed to have a girlfriend.' He laughed again. 'They used to call him Pixie, the other kids in the street, he had very small, pointed ears.' He finished his beer and Lambert signalled the girl to bring him another.

'He had quite a bit of property in Cannonbridge at one time, from what he told me,' Lambert said.

'Took after his father in that. His father was an insurance agent but he dabbled in property on the side. He had eight or ten houses put out to rent, small working-class houses. Vincent followed him into the insurance business when he left school, his Dad got him a job in the same office. He still lived at home with his parents.' Udell started on his second beer with relish.

'His wife seems a pleasant enough woman,' Lambert observed.

'Wife?' Udell echoed on a note of astonishment. 'He's never gone and got married?'

'He's been married a couple of years.'

'Well, well, well.' Udell's tone took on an edge of irony and malice. 'So he finally took the plunge. I wonder how long it'll last.' He saw Lambert's look. 'Bit of a rum bugger, our Vincent,' he said with relish. 'There was that bit of trouble a while back—fourteen or fifteen years ago now, must be. He'd be coming up to forty then, tricky age for a single man.'

'What trouble was that?' Lambert asked casually.

Udell smiled like a man contemplating a particularly juicy morsel. 'That business with the girls.' He grinned again. 'I don't suppose he advertises that in Cannonbridge along with his double glazing.'

'What did he get up to?'

'Touching up young girls, children really. Both his parents were dead by then, his father first, and then his mother a year or two later. He was still living in the same house, on his own. It would be a couple of years after his mother died that it all came out. He'd taken over all his father's property and of course he did the rounds regularly, calling for the rent or taking a look at something that needed repair. And of course sometimes the parents would be out, it would just be one of the kids at home.' He gave Lambert a knowing look. 'I don't need to spell it out, you can imagine the sort of thing. Probably been getting away with it for God knows how long. But then there were a couple of cases—'

'Court cases?'

'No, they never came to court. Apparently he'd been handing out sweets, bits of presents, money, enough to keep the kids' mouths shut. But one of the kids finally started talking. The father went rampaging round to see Vincent, breathing fire, threatening death and destruction. Vincent paid him off.' He brooded over the crumbs of his chicken pie. 'Word got round and two or three other fathers started questioning their kids. Vincent had a few more visitors and he had to shell out some more cash. Then the rumours really started to fly and some of them reached the insurance company. He had to resign. He put all his Tappenhall property on the market and cleared out.'

He drained his glass and set it down. He settled back in his chair and began to yawn. His face was a trifle flushed, his eyes had a glazed, sleepy look. Beside him on the table the pile of pamphlets lay untouched.

Lambert stood up. 'I've got to be pushing off,' he said. 'But there's no need for you to disturb yourself. I'll get you another beer.' He signalled to the girl. 'I'll let you know about the holiday.'

The rain had stopped and a tremulous sunlight was beginning to filter through the clouds by the time Lambert reached the nursing home; it appeared to be sunk into a peaceful afternoon somnolence. He rang the bell and inquired for the matron. When she appeared he disclosed his identity and asked if there was a Mr Minshull living at the home. She told him there was, he had been there over two years.

'I wonder if I might have a word with him,' Lambert said. 'It's possible he might be able to give us some information about a case I'm working on.'

'It'll be that dreadful business about the two girls,' Matron said at once. 'Mr Minshull read about it in the papers. It was most upsetting for him, having known one of the girls.'

'I'll do my best not to upset him any further,' Lambert promised. 'I won't keep him long. Just one or two straight-forward questions.'

'I think he's over it now,' she told him. 'But I'm afraid he's gone downhill a good deal in the last two years. It's his memory mostly. On his good days he's able to read the papers and listen to the radio, he can follow what's going on in the world. But on his bad days—' She sighed and shook her head. 'He can't concentrate on anything, he gets very depressed. He's not too bad today, he was brighter at lunch. He's in the sun lounge now, he likes to sit there in the afternoon.'

She led the way down a passage into a long glazed-in room looking out over the tranquil, subjugated spaces of the garden, fresh and sparkling now after the rain. At one end of the lounge an old woman lay back in a reclining chair, fast asleep. At the other end an old man, very thin and frail-looking, sat reading a book with a rug tucked in round him. He glanced up as they came over. His face was almost fleshless, his eyes sunk into deep pits. Pale skin, covered with brown blotches, stretched tight over his cheekbones. The few strands of white hair that covered the polished dome of his head were neatly trimmed and brushed. He looked at them from watery, pale blue eyes.

'I don't want you to get upset,' Matron told him in a soothing voice. 'It's nothing to agitate yourself about. This gentleman is from the Cannonbridge police. He believes you may be able to help them with some information about that poor girl.'

'Helen Mowbray,' Minshull said. He didn't appear alarmed or perturbed.

Lambert asked him if Joanne Mowbray had made any kind of contact with him. Minshull shook his head. Lambert glanced at Matron. No, she knew of no visit, no phone call or letter from Joanne. 'I expect you'd like to talk in private,' she said. 'I'll look in again shortly.'

'Pull up a chair,' Minshull said to Lambert when she had gone. 'I'm afraid there isn't much I can tell you.'

Lambert asked if he had any idea where Helen might have gone after leaving the flat. 'I'm afraid not,' Minshull said. 'We weren't on those sort of terms. She was a nicely-mannered girl, always very civil when our paths crossed, but we both valued our privacy. Neither of us was the type to exchange confidences.'

'We're trying to discover if she had any special friends at that time, particularly men friends.'

He shook his head slowly. 'I'm afraid I don't know about any men friends. I never saw any, or knew about any calling at Holmwood, but then I wouldn't expect to. It was a solidly built house, not the modern kind where you can hear your neighbour sneeze. The two parts of the house were quite separate—and in any case I'm not a nosy person. I wasn't much interested in what she was doing, I was always busy

with my writing. I lived very quietly and my impression was
that she did the same.'

'Did that surprise you? A good-looking young woman?'

He considered. 'I suppose it might, if I'd given the matter
any thought.' He smiled suddenly. 'The only man I can
remember calling was the landlord, Mr Udell. He often
called. I pulled her leg about it once or twice—that was when
I was arranging with her about the cat. She was very good
about my cat. I used to go away sometimes for a day or two to
my married sister's and Helen used to feed the cat, she'd
made friends with it in the garden. I remember saying to her:
I do believe Udell's sweet on you.'

'What did she say to that?'

'She just laughed, she didn't take offence. She said she did
some work for Udell, secretarial work, accounts, that was
all.'

'Did she strike you as lonely?'

'No, not a bit. Self-sufficient, yes, but not lonely. I understood that, I'm very much that way inclined myself.'

'Do you know if she had any women friends?'

'I don't remember any woman calling at the flat.' He
raised a hand suddenly. 'Oh—there was that day when she
was all dressed up, she had a flowery hat on. I was in the
garden and she came out, ready to go off somewhere. I said:
You look as if you're going to a wedding. She said: That's
exactly where I am going. I said they'd picked the right day
for a wedding. It was brilliant sunshine, a lovely June day,
the birds were singing, all the roses out. She said it was a
country wedding, a girl she knew from the last place she'd
worked at, she was marrying a farmer. She laughed and said:
Good name for a farmer, too.'

'Did she tell you what his name was? Or where he lived?'

'She didn't say where he lived but she did say his name. I
can remember smiling and saying, Yes, a very suitable name
for a farmer.'

'Can you remember what the name was?'

Minshull frowned and sighed. After a few moments he shook his head. 'I'm sorry, I'm afraid it's gone.'

'Field?' Lambert suggested. 'Meadows? Haycock?'

Minshull shook his head again.

'Shepherd? Grazier?'

Minshull began to look agitated, he started to bite his lip.

'Bullock? Hogg?'

He drew a quavering breath and turned his head from side to side. As if summoned by invisible impulses Matron suddenly appeared in the doorway. She cast a piercing glance in their direction. At the sight of Minshull's puckered face she came swiftly over, flinging Lambert a glance of keen reproach. 'It's all right,' he assured her. 'I'm just leaving.'

He got to his feet. 'Don't worry about it,' he told Minshull. He leaned down and touched the old man's thin knotted hand with its wrinkled, papery skin and prominent blue veins. 'Thank you for your help, you've been of great assistance.'

Minshull's face cleared suddenly. He glanced up at Lambert with a smile. 'Stockman!' he said in triumph. 'A very good name for a farmer.'

Chief Inspector Kelsey sat at his desk studying the map of Holmwood that Vincent Udell had dropped in at the station earlier in the morning. The map was painstakingly drawn with an eye for scale, attention to detail; the work of a man at home in the world of property.

He looked up from the map and sat drumming his fingers on the desk. It seemed highly unlikely now, after a lapse of two and a half years, that they would ever be able to uncover the exact time or other precise details of Helen Mowbray's death, but he had every hope of being able to do so in Joanne's case. It seemed very probable that Joanne had met her death on the evening of Wednesday, March 2nd; they had come across no sighting or contact after that date.

But the motive for Helen's murder remained of paramount importance, the key to both crimes. When we know that, he thought, we'll be more than half way home.

According to Udell, it was on a Friday that Helen had left Holmwood: November 28th. Nowhere among her belongings was there anything to provide an indication of where she had intended going. There were few papers of any kind; no photographs, nothing of a personal nature. There were some business receipts relating to work she had done for various tradesmen in the last few months before her death; Udell's name appeared on some of these. Every tradesman on the agency list had now been interviewed but nothing remotely resembling a lead had been uncovered.

It seemed very probable that Helen had been killed on November 28th; they had found no trace of her after that date.

He turned his attention again to the map. There were a number of fair-sized old houses strung out along one side of Tappenhall Road; on the opposite side was a stretch of open land. Holmwood had been the last house in the road, standing on the edge of town. Beyond it lay a furniture depository and an area of scrub, leading on to the industrial estate. On the far side of the estate was a certain amount of residential development arising from the industrial expansion.

Next to Holmwood on the side nearest the town was a shop with living accommodation; the property now stood empty. It had belonged to a widow who had run the shop for many years as a general store, struggling on against changing shopping habits and her own declining forces until her death twelve months ago. The property was still up for sale in a sluggish market.

The ground in the area had a pronounced slope and Holmwood, like many of the other dwellings, had been built with two floors at the front and three at the back. The basement flat, which Helen had occupied, could be entered by two exterior doors, one at the back and the other facing the blank wall of the depository. Between the depository and Holmwood a narrow alley ran down from the Tappenhall Road to another road a hundred and twenty yards below. The rear garden of Holmwood was surrounded on three sides by a high brick wall with a door leading into the alley. A visitor wishing to escape notice could leave a car on the lower road and walk unobserved up the alley and in through the garden.

Helen had opened a current account at a Cannonbridge bank shortly after arriving in the town. She had maintained the account without trouble or incident, had never been overdrawn, had never asked for a loan. Her last transaction was a few days before she left Holmwood; she had said nothing to the bank about any change of address. There had been no further movement in the account and the bank had heard nothing more from her.

In one of her suitcases was an envelope containing a number of Government savings certificates and bonds, all of which could be bought over the counter—for cash if need be—at any post office; all were tax exempt and required no explanation to the Inland Revenue. Her first purchase had been made some three years ago and her last a fortnight before she left Holmwood. The purchases had been made at irregular intervals and for irregular amounts, one or two of them sizeable.

There was no record of any will. It seemed likely that all Helen's savings would eventually find their way into the coffers of the State.

Shortly after six there was a phone call for the Chief from a Mrs Cope, speaking from an address in Wychford, a small town ten miles to the west of Cannonbridge. She had been away over Easter, had got back home a couple of hours ago, had picked up the local paper and read about the murders.

'I thought I'd better phone right away,' she told Kelsey. 'I knew Helen Mowbray slightly—very slightly, really, but I think you may be interested in the circumstances.'

'What were the circumstances?' he asked.

'I met her at an abortion clinic. Two years ago last September.'

CHAPTER 8

Mrs Cope lived with her two children in a red-brick semi, tall and narrow, in an avenue on the outskirts of Wychford. She had sent the children off out of the way, to play with schoolfriends a couple of streets away. She was still in the middle of unpacking after the weekend, carrying a load of holiday washing down to a utility room in the basement, when the two policemen arrived at the front door half an hour after she had phoned. She came running up from the basement when Lambert pressed the bell.

'Sorry the place is in such a mess,' she said. A tall, slim woman, thirty-six or -seven. No make-up; good-looking enough, eyes like clear brown water, long chestnut hair whisked up on top of her head and tied with a bootlace. She wore jeans and a sweater, the sleeves pushed up to her elbows. She had a swift, direct gaze, an air of habitual tension.

She took them into a big, old-fashioned kitchen. 'I just sat down for a moment,' she told them, 'and picked up the paper. There it was, on the front page.' She drew a long breath. 'I couldn't believe it.' She suddenly bethought herself. 'Would you like some tea? Or coffee? I could do with a cup myself.'

Kelsey settled for tea. 'I've been over at my mother's,' she said as she filled the kettle. 'She's getting on, she hasn't been at all well this last year or two. She likes to see the kids.' She put the kettle on to boil and dropped into a chair. A moment later she sprang up again and snatched a packet of cigarettes from the dresser. She offered them but both men shook their heads.

'Very wise,' she said with a loud sigh. 'I did give them up a few years back but I took it up again, what with the divorce and everything.'

'If you could tell us about your acquaintance with Helen Mowbray,' Kelsey said.

She jumped up again to make the tea. 'We both had abortions at the same clinic.' She mentioned the name of a private establishment some sixty miles away. 'I couldn't really afford to go private but I wanted to get it done quickly, without anyone local knowing.' She set the teapot down on the table, took milk from the fridge, beakers from the dresser. 'It was when the solicitors were arguing about the alimony. My husband was being very stroppy about it, he didn't want me to have a penny.' She pulled a face. 'If he'd got wind of the abortion—you can just imagine.' She poured the tea. 'It wasn't as if I'd got pregnant because of some marvellous love-affair. I scarcely knew the man. It was just a moment of madness, no real relationship or anything, just a guy I met. I was so damned fed up with everything just then.' She pushed the beakers across the table to them. 'Helen had hers done the same day as me. We were going home on the same train so we shared a taxi, travelled together.' She began to drink her tea.

'Did she tell you much about herself?'

'She didn't say a lot then, not coming back in the train. You don't feel like pouring out your life story when you've just come out of one of those places.' She made a little grimace. 'It's a bit of a shock to the system. But as far as I could make out she seemed to be on her own, to have no family. I asked her if there was anyone to keep an eye on her when she got home and she said no, she lived by herself in a flat, the only other tenant was an old man. I felt sorry for her so I gave her this address and said why didn't she give me a

ring and come over for a meal and a chat some time if she
fancied it, if she felt blue. I told her what my own situation
was.'

'Did she take you up on that?'

'Yes, she came over a few times. She drove over in her
car—'

'Car?' Kelsey echoed sharply.

'Yes, she had a little blue Triumph Spitfire, a nice little
car, very sporty.'

'Do you know if it was her own car?'

'I didn't actually ask her about it but I certainly had the
impression it belonged to her.'

'Did she say anything about getting rid of the car?'

'No, she never mentioned anything like that. I passed a
remark about the car the first time she came over and she
talked about it then. She said it was a nippy little vehicle,
more economical than you might think. She seemed happy
enough with it. She used to stay to lunch when she came and
then she'd go back in the afternoon, when my children came
in from school. The last time she came over, that would be at
the end of October, my mother had gone into hospital for an
operation a few days before. My mother lives in a cottage
miles away from here, in the depths of the country. I couldn't
go running over there to look after her when she came out of
hospital so I said she'd better come here to convalesce. I told
Helen I wouldn't be able to see her for the next month or two,
I'd be up to my eyes. She said she'd give me a ring in a few
weeks to see how I was fixed.' She drew on her cigarette. 'I
never heard from her again.'

'Were you surprised?'

'No, not really. I was so busy I didn't have time to give her
a thought. My mother took a lot longer to get over the
operation than I'd expected. When she finally did go back
home—that wasn't till after Christmas—and I had time to
draw breath again, I thought about Helen then once or
twice, I wondered why she'd never rung. I thought: Oh well,

ships that pass in the night. She's probably getting over the abortion now, wants to put it all behind her. Coming over here would only remind her of it.' She stubbed out her cigarette with force and glanced up at Kelsey. 'And all that time she was—' She gave a little shudder. 'Doesn't bear thinking about.' She flicked a tear from her cheek.

'How did she strike you?' Kelsey asked. 'Would you think she was a girl who'd go overboard if she fell in love?'

She shook her head. 'Far from it. I couldn't see her going overboard for anyone. She struck me as a very level-headed type, all out for number one.' She moved her head. 'Of course that might have had something to do with the abortion, it could have made her hard.'

'Was she still seeing the man responsible?'

'I didn't ask her, she said very little about herself. I've had enough hassle myself to understand her wanting to keep her private life private. But from one or two little things, I did definitely get the impression she was still involved with the same man.'

'Did she appear to resent what had happened? To feel he'd let her down?'

'I never got that impression. She seemed to take it all pretty philosophically. You should have seen some of the girls at the clinic, they were really shattered by it, some of them were very bitter. But Helen seemed to look on it all in a very matter-of-fact way—a pity it happened, but she had to go through with it so there was no use making a fuss.'

'There was no question of the man marrying her?'

'I did say something about that once but she just shook her head and made a face, as if it was totally out of the question. I assumed he was married already or else she wasn't keen on the idea of marriage herself—she certainly didn't strike me as a girl who'd want to get married.'

'Do you know if the man paid for the abortion?'

'I happened to mention once about the abortion being very expensive, how I had to pay for it myself, there was no question of the man paying, he was just a fly-by-night. She said: I came out of the money side of it all right, I made very sure of that. Two boyfriends, two handouts. I couldn't help saying: I suppose you do know which of them was the father? She said: Oh, I know all right, and so does he. But it was just about possible it could have been the other one—or at least I made him think it was. She laughed and said: It didn't do Master Blue Eyes any harm at all to have a damn good fright. Anyway, he could afford it, his nest's well feathered. I suppose she saw I didn't look very approving. She said: Well, why not? They exploit us, we exploit them. I don't see why all the exploiting should be on one side.

'I asked her if the two men knew about each other. She said: Hardly, I'm not that much of a fool. Anyway, Master Blue Eyes isn't around any more. He had a fit when he heard the word abortion. He gave me the money and that's the last I saw of him. Or ever will see. She said he never even phoned after she got back from the clinic, to ask how she was. But she didn't seem to mind, she was half-laughing when she talked about it.'

'The other man,' Kelsey said, 'the one responsible for the pregnancy, could he afford to hand over the abortion fee?'

'I got the impression he was well heeled too. She had a bracelet on one day when she came over. It looked pretty valuable. She said he'd given it to her a few months back, in the summer.'

'Can you describe the bracelet?' Kelsey asked with sharp interest. Among Helen's possessions were few trinkets of any kind and only one piece of jewellery worth the name: an antique bracelet in a velvet-lined box; the box bore no jeweller's name. The bracelet was fashioned from slender gold chains secured at intervals with narrow vertical strips of finely chased gold, set with turquoises and seed pearls.

'Yes, I remember it very well,' Mrs Cope told him. 'I admired it and she took it off to show me. It was really beautiful, she said it was quite old. I slipped it on my wrist. It was made of gold chains with gold bars holding the chains together. The bars were set with stones, pearls and turquoises.'

'Did she never mention this man's name?'

'No, never. I used to think how cagey she was. The nearest she ever came to using a name was when she called the other boyfriend Master Blue Eyes.'

Joanne Mowbray had made no kind of contact with Mrs Cope.

'When I read the paper,' she said, 'I was astonished to see that Helen had a sister—and a stepbrother. I never knew she had any family.'

Shortly after returning to the station they had the information about Helen Mowbray's Triumph Spitfire. Among the details were some that caused Kelsey to sit chewing his lips. The car had been sold to a dealer in a village five miles the other side of Wychford, two days before Helen vacated the flat; six weeks later the dealer broke the car for scrap. The name of the person who had owned the car immediately before Helen was David Bartram Hinckley.

And the date on which the car had passed from Hinckley to Helen was three months after Helen had left Wyatt's, three months since—according to what Hinckley had told them—he had last had any kind of contact, any kind of dealing with her.

The breaker's yard extended over half an acre of rough ground on the outskirts of the village; its more unlovely aspects were screened from the passing gaze by a belt of tall, thickly grown trees. Behind the trees a stout wooden fence, six feet high, reinforced with barbed wire, bore a large notice prominently displayed: WARNING: STAY CLEAR. GUARD DOGS PATROL THIS SITE.

They were certainly not patrolling the site when Lambert drove up at eight-thirty on Friday morning; they were fast

asleep after their night's exertions. He spotted them as he
followed Kelsey across the site; he glanced inside an old
Bedford van body and saw, down on the floor of the van, two
large, powerful-looking, dark-coated German shepherd dogs
comfortably stretched out cheek by jowl on a deep bed of
straw.

Kelsey made his way between rows of cars in various
stages of decrepitude and dissection. The dealer was expecting them; according to one of the young men at work
stripping the vehicles, he was in his office in the middle of the
yard.

He came out at the sound of their approach. A lean, sinewy
man with a shrewd, amiable face, bony hands permanently
grimed and stained.

'Terrible business,' he said. 'I didn't know anything about
it till you rang. I've been looking out my records,' he added
as he led the way back inside his office. 'And taking a look at
the newspapers.' His office was small and crowded. On top of
his littered desk lay a couple of newspapers and an open
ledger. He gestured at the newspapers. 'I'd heard there'd
been some nasty murders over at Stoneleigh but I've never
been one to bother reading about such things, too much to
do. We're up to the eyeballs here at this time of year, as soon
as the weather starts improving.'

Kelsey asked if Joanne Mowbray had made contact with
him but he shook his head; there had been no inquiry of any
kind.

He showed the Chief the entry in the ledger. 'You didn't
give her much for the car,' Kelsey observed.

'Spitfire Mark 3,' the dealer said. 'F registration. It hadn't
been looked after, it had been knocked about. It would never
have passed its next MOT. It didn't warrant spending
anything on it, I'd never have got it back.'

'You seem to remember the car all right,' Kelsey said. 'Do
you remember the girl?'

'I've been thinking about it since you rang. I remember

the place, out on the Tappenhall Road, basement flat. And I remember the girl, dark hair, good figure. Smart girl too, didn't waste time flannelling, telling me what a marvellous little car it was, how it broke her heart to part with it. She just said she wanted it out of the way, what would I give her for it?'

'Did she say anything about her plans? Why she was selling the car?'

He frowned down at the desk. 'I don't remember her saying anything about her plans. She did say she was getting another car. She'd phoned me in the morning, that would be November the twenty-sixth, to say she had a car she wanted to sell. I told her I'd be over in the afternoon. She was waiting for me, we struck a bargain. I paid her in cash. We didn't stand about chatting, I wasn't there above ten minutes.'

'Did you notice anything about her state of mind? If she seemed worried or nervous?'

'Far from it. She seemed in a good mood.' He tilted back his head and closed his eyes. 'Pleased with herself, as if she'd pulled off a tricky deal.' He flashed a sharp look at the Chief. 'Nothing to do with selling me the car, you saw what I gave her for it. A fair price for what it was, but no more than the scrap value.' He waved a hand. 'Not that I'd have tried to do her in any case. A hard nut to crack, that's how she struck me.'

David Hinckley's studio stood in the garden of Grayshott Manor, a few yards from the rear of the house. A well-proportioned, elegant structure, designed and built with only a fleeting eye to expense.

On this fine spring morning Hinckley went across to the studio as usual, after breakfasting with Julia Wyatt. His secretary, who came in five mornings a week, had already arrived; she was in the office, opening the mail. He was busy dictating letters to her when the housekeeper brought Chief Inspector Kelsey and Sergeant Lambert over to the studio.

The Chief ran his eye over the secretary. She looked ferociously competent, personally chosen for the post, he would have been prepared to wager, by Julia Wyatt. She was certainly of an age, shape and general appearance calculated to set that lady's mind at rest when she departed every morning for one or other of the Wyatt branches.

The Chief also observed that while Hinckley didn't appear overjoyed to see them, he didn't appear surprised. He took them into a reception room adjoining the office and offered them refreshments, which Kelsey declined.

'You told us definitely and categorically the other day that you had no contact, no dealings of any kind with Helen Mowbray after she left Wyatt's,' Kelsey said abruptly when they were all three seated. Hinckley gave a nod. His eyes were disciplined and wary; he sat on the edge of his chair in a rigid, alert posture.

'Do you stand by that?' Kelsey asked. Again Hinckley nodded.

'Then how do you account for the fact that three months after Helen left Wyatt's, three months after you had any kind of contact with her, both you and she registered change of ownership of a blue Triumph Spitfire, a change of ownership from you to her?'

Hinckley got to his feet and walked across to the window. He stood looking out at a magnificent magnolia bush a few feet away, its great white flowers stained with purple. 'I did have some brief contact with her,' he said. 'I didn't think you'd be concerned with anything as slight as that. She knew I was getting another car. She liked the Triumph, she'd asked me if I'd sell it to her when I got the new car. I told her I would. I got the new car three months after she left. I rang her and fixed the deal.' He turned from the window. 'That was all.'

'You sold her the car?'

'Yes.'

'Sold it or made her a present of it?'

'I sold it,' Hinckley said shortly.

'For how much?'

He raised his shoulders. His eyes began their rapid blink. 'I can't remember the exact figure, not offhand. The same as I'd have got for it as a trade-in, I expect. I certainly wasn't out to fleece her. It wasn't worth much, it was pretty clapped out.'

'You keep your bank statements?' Kelsey asked.

'Yes.' The rate of blinking increased.

'Then they will show the amount of the cheque she gave you for the car. We'll wait while you look it up.'

'I don't believe she did give me a cheque,' Hinckley said after a brief silence. 'I think she paid me in cash.'

'Why was that?'

He pulled down the corners of his mouth. 'I didn't ask, none of my business.'

'And after this transaction did you resume your relationship?'

'No.'

'Not by any kind of contact, however slight or brief?'

Hinckley shook his head with resolution.

'You would swear to that in court?'

'I would.'

Kelsey studied him in silence; he remained motionless and tense under the scrutiny. 'Were you responsible for the pregnancy which caused her to have an abortion eleven months after she left Wyatt's?' Kelsey asked suddenly.

There was another, longer silence. Hinckley clasped his hands behind his back and stared down at the floor.

'I can see your difficulty,' Kelsey observed in a detached tone. 'You've a shrewd idea that we know you gave Helen the money for her abortion, but you've just told us you're ready to swear you had no contact with her for eight months before she went into the clinic.' Hinckley still said nothing. 'I suggest it's time to cut out the fairy stories,' Kelsey said, 'and start telling us the truth.'

Hinckley exhaled a long breath. He raised his head and looked at the Chief.

'You maintained the relationship with Helen after she left Wyatt's,' Kelsey said in a brisker tone.

Hinckley's eyes began again their compulsive blinking. 'I didn't see all that much of her. I was never in love with her, it was just a casual relationship.'

'Did she do any accounts for you?'

He looked startled. 'No, she didn't.'

'Not at any time?'

'No, never.'

'She didn't, for instance, help you to doctor the accounts you presented to Mrs Wyatt?'

'She did nothing of the sort,' Hinckley said brusquely. 'I don't fiddle the books.'

'Maybe you don't now,' Kelsey said. 'Maybe you don't need to. But maybe you fiddled them then, and maybe Helen assisted you.'

'That's utter rubbish,' Hinckley said with force. 'There was never anything like that.'

'Did she tell you you were responsible for her pregnancy?'

There was an appreciable pause before Hinckley answered. Finally he said, 'Yes, she did, but I didn't believe her. I hadn't even seen her for a couple of months.'

'Have you any idea who her other men friends might have been?'

'No idea at all.'

'Did you ever try to find out?'

He looked surprised. 'No, never. It wouldn't occur to me.'

'Do you consider yourself a possessive or jealous man?'

A flicker of distaste crossed Hinckley's face. 'I certainly do not.'

'Even though you didn't believe you were responsible for her pregnancy, you did in fact pay for the abortion?' Hinckley nodded. 'Why was that?'

'I didn't want her going to see Julia—Mrs Wyatt.'

'Did she threaten to?'

'Not in so many words. But it was there in her manner.'

'Did you argue with her about it? Did you deny responsibility? Say you wouldn't pay?'

'I did to begin with, but we both knew she had me over a barrel.'

'How much did you give her?'

'I gave her what she asked for, it struck me as pretty steep.' He mentioned a sum exactly twice what Mrs Cope had told them the clinic had charged her. 'I knew she was laying it on but I wasn't in any position to haggle.'

'In what form was the money handed over?'

'In cash.'

'By your wish or hers?'

'It suited both of us.'

'Were you paying the rent of her flat?'

'I was not,' he said with emphasis.

'Did you ever pay the rent of her flat?'

'I did not.'

'Or assist with the rent?'

There was another pause. 'I wouldn't exactly call it that,' he said at last.

'You helped with one or two living expenses?'

'That was more like it.'

'What sort of amounts are we talking about?'

His face took on a stubborn look. 'Not a great deal.'

'Could you be more precise?'

The look deepened. 'I'm afraid not, after all this time. It varied, but it was never very much.'

'In what form were these sums handed over?'

'In cash.'

'Did you give Helen a gold bracelet?'

He shook his head. 'I never gave her any jewellery.'

'After the abortion, did she ask you for more money?'

'No.'

'She made no attempt to blackmail you over the abortion?'

'No, never.'

'Did that surprise you?'

Hinckley said nothing for some time. At last he said, 'It did, rather.'

'Did she know about your promotion? That Mrs Wyatt had invited you to live at the Manor?'

'As far as I'm aware, she didn't know. I certainly never told her.'

'And now,' Kelsey said crisply, 'if we could have the truth: Exactly when did you last have any kind of contact with Helen? However slight or fleeting?'

'When I gave her the money for the abortion,' Hinckley said at once. The blinking had ceased. 'I didn't want any more to do with her after that, I knew I'd been taken for a ride.' He paused and added, 'Julia doesn't know about any of this. She doesn't know there was any association after Helen left Wyatt's.' Kelsey said nothing. 'There's no reason, surely,' Hinckley said on a note of appeal, 'why she should know about it now?'

Kelsey made no response. Instead he asked, 'What is the situation here between you and Mrs Wyatt?'

Hinckley moved a hand. 'We live together.'

'Is there any thought of marriage?'

'Not at present,' he answered in a tone devoid of expression.

'Have you asked her to marry you?'

He closed his eyes briefly. 'Yes, I have.'

'And she refused?'

'She said things could continue as they are for the present.' After a moment he said again, 'There's no reason, surely, why she should know anything about all this?'

'She won't hear of it from me,' Kelsey said brusquely. He sat back in his chair. 'Wednesday March 2nd. Where were you from, say, three o'clock that afternoon?'

He frowned. 'I can't say offhand. I should have to look it up.'

'Then look it up.'

He took a diary from his pocket and turned the pages. 'I went over to the factory after lunch,' he said after a minute or two. 'I was there till half past five. I got back here about six-fifteen.'

'Was Mrs Wyatt here when you got back?'

'No, she'd been over to one of the other branches. She got back just in time to change before we went out. We were going to a charity fashion show.' He mentioned the time and place, the name of the organization. 'We left here at about a quarter to eight. We went to the show with some friends and afterwards we went home with them for an hour or two.' Again he supplied details. 'It was after twelve by the time we got back here. We went straight to bed.'

'Did you spend any part of that afternoon or evening with Joanne Mowbray?'

He shook his head with force. 'I didn't even know she existed.'

'She hadn't been in touch with you?'

'She had not.'

'You hadn't arranged to meet her during Wednesday afternoon?'

'I had not.' He looked steadily back at the Chief.

'Stoneleigh,' Kelsey said. 'The derelict property by the motorway, where the bodies were found. You know the spot?'

He shook his head.

'It's only a matter of five or six miles from here.'

Hinckley said nothing.

'You must drive past there every time you go to the factory.'

He jerked his head impatiently. 'I have no interest in derelict properties. It would never occur to me to notice it.'

Kelsey regarded him in silence. Finally he said, 'Are you a local man?'

'No, not exactly.'

'Where do you come from?'

'From Wychford.'

'Not a bad little town,' Kelsey observed. 'Some parts of it are very pleasant.' Hinckley remained silent. 'Which part do you come from?' Kelsey asked with bland persistence.

A look of irritation crossed Hinckley's face. 'Flatley Road,' he said shortly. 'By the common.'

'Your family still live over there?'

'My parents are dead. I have no relatives now in the town.'

Kelsey stood up. 'I'd like a word with your secretary before we go.'

Hinckley gave him an abstracted glance. 'Yes, by all means.'

'No need to trouble yourself,' Kelsey said as Hinckley made to accompany them. 'We won't keep her a moment.'

The secretary was busy typing when Kelsey came into the office. 'If we might ask you one or two questions,' he said.

She gave a nod of acquiescence, she seemed in no way surprised.

'Did you have a visit or a phone call here a few weeks ago from Joanne Mowbray?'

'No, we had neither.' Again she appeared not at all surprised.

'You recognize the name?'

'Yes, she was one of those two girls at Stoneleigh.'

'Did you ever hear her name mentioned here—before you read about her in the newspapers?'

She shook her head.

'How long have you worked here?'

'Ever since Mr Hinckley began working from here. It's more than two years now.'

'Where did you work before?'

'I always worked at Wyatt's until a few years ago, then my husband became very ill and I had to leave, to nurse him. After he died I wrote to Mrs Wyatt to say I'd like to go back to work again. I asked her if she had anything for me. She offered me this. I work here in the mornings, and at the Cannonbridge branch in the afternoons.'

She sat calm and unruffled, waiting for the next question, but all he said was, 'Thank you for your help.'

As they walked across to the car Kelsey looked at his watch; he had to get back to the station. 'Whistle me up another car,' he instructed Lambert. 'Then you can get over to Wychford, have a nose round Flatley Road. After that you can call in at the flat Hinckley lived in in Cannonbridge, before he moved out here, see if there's anything to be got there. Don't take all day about it—I want another word with Vincent Udell some time today.'

CHAPTER 9

I doubt if Hinckley would recognize his old stamping ground now, Lambert thought as he stood surveying the houses in Flatley Road. The area appeared to have undergone a massive if haphazard facelift in recent times. A considerable amount of infill building had also taken place, tiny new houses and minute bungalows being squeezed into the gardens of existing houses, the majority of which had been re-roofed, freshly rendered, furnished with new windows and doors.

Extensions and porches had been added wherever there was a spare foot of space, and the whole decorated in a rainbow medley of markedly individual colour schemes. The end result was spirited, to say the least, an eloquent testimonial to the Englishman's urge to do something, anything, to a property the moment it passes into his hands, and every spring thereafter.

Even the corner newsagent's—one of Lambert's old reliable standbys when it came to inquiring about local residents—had changed hands within the last year or two and had consequently been enlarged, smartened up, hideously decorated, and then stocked to the eaves with ice-cream, T-shirts, toys and videos, leaving scarcely an inch of room for newspapers and magazines.

Lambert pushed open the door without hope, and without hope inquired about the Hinckleys. Even before he had finished his spiel, heads were being shaken at the other side of the counter. Sorry, wouldn't know, newcomers here ourselves; he might try the pub in the next street or the post office a quarter of a mile away. He left the shop and stood outside on the pavement, pondering his next move.

As he glanced irresolutely about, a spry old man came out of a house some way up the road, one of the few houses that had so far escaped the relentless hands of the transformers; a little Yorkshire terrier trotted docilely along beside him. The two of them set off up the road at a good steady pace.

Lambert hastened after them; as he caught up he could hear the old man chatting animatedly to the dog. He made his apologies and once more began his spiel: he was trying to trace a family who had lived in Flatley Road some years ago—perhaps the old man could help him?

The old man came to a halt, with the Yorkie obediently to heel. 'If I can't help you, no one can,' he declared stoutly. 'I was born in Flatley Road, brought up here, married here, raised my family here. I shall very likely die here. Which family was it you wanted?'

'Name of Hinckley.'

The old man threw back his head and laughed. 'Hinckley! I should say I do remember them. They lived two doors down from me. A lively lot, they were, good-looking, too. The street was a lot duller after the last of them left.' He broke off. 'Mind if we walk along to the common? We can chat as we go. I take my little Yorkie over there three or four times a day, she looks forward to her jaunts.'

'By all means,' Lambert said. 'It's good of you to spare me the time.'

'Time's one thing I have got to spare these days,' the old man said cheerfully as they set off again. 'I've got reams and reams of it. A dog's good company when you're on your own, someone to talk to, stops you going round the twist.' He looked up at Lambert. 'I talk back to the radio and TV these days.' He grinned. 'They tell me that's a bad sign.'

'Did you know the Hinckleys well?' Lambert asked.

'Pretty well. The girls were of an age with my own family. Two girls and a boy, I had, they went to school with the Hinckleys. The Hinckleys had four girls. They kept trying for a lad and they managed it in the end, there was great rejoicing when he was born. And then poor Hinckley went and had a stroke when the lad was barely twelve months old. He fell down unconscious one morning in the bank, when he was serving a customer at the counter. He was no age at all, forty-three or -four at the outside. He never regained consciousness, he was dead inside a week. Very hardworking chap always, terrific worrier.' The flood of talk poured from him, inexhaustible, unstoppable. 'His wife was just the opposite, big and jolly. She had a hard time of it after he died—different days then, they didn't give you all these social security handouts like they do now, and she only had a miserable little pension from the bank. But she didn't sit about moaning. She'd always made the girls' clothes, so she started taking in dressmaking. The two eldest girls helped her a lot, they turned out very handy with a needle. They all rubbed along well enough.'

They reached the main road and crossed over to a stretch of common land with benches dotted here and there. The old man made for his accustomed seat. He took a ball from his pocket and the rest of his conversation with Lambert was punctuated by yaps and barks from the Yorkie and encouraging cries from the old man as he flung the ball for the terrier to retrieve.

'The Hinckleys were a very nice family.' He laughed again. 'What a fuss they made of that lad! You'd think no family had ever had a boy before. Petted and cosseted and dressed up like a little doll, he was, when he was in the pram. I used to wonder sometimes what way he'd turn out, brought up in a houseful of females. He was a good-looking lad—and a vain one too, very fond of looking at himself in the mirror. When he finished school he went off to art college; studying fashion design, he told me. Hardly surprising, living in that house. Any time you dropped in, the place was full of ribbons and flounces. One of the girls would be cutting something out and another would be running something up on the machine. David—that was the lad's name—he was used to giving them a hand from the time he could pick a pin up off the floor.'

He sighed. 'Mrs Hinckley took ill and died soon after David went off to college, and then the girls started getting married, one by one. They're scattered all round the county now. I haven't seen young David for years. I've no idea where he is or what he's doing.' He grinned. 'One thing I'm willing to bet, though: wherever he is, he's still being cosseted by some woman.'

The flat in which David Hinckley had been living before he moved out to Grayshott Manor was in a tree-lined road in a residential suburb of Cannonbridge. There were several sizable Victorian houses in the road, well kept, with trim front gardens; the address Hinckley had given them was of a first-floor flat in one of these houses.

Lambert found the communal front door unlocked. He went inside, into a spacious, well-proportioned hall with an ornate ceiling and fine cornice work. He went up the stairs to the first floor and pressed the bell several times without response. From the ground-floor flat he heard the sound of a vacuum cleaner starting up. He went down and pressed the bell there. The sound of the cleaner ceased and a smart-looking woman in her early sixties came to the door.

Lambert disclosed his identity but not the case on which

he was working. The woman's manner was friendly and cooperative. No, there was no one at home in the first-floor flat; the married couple who lived there both worked in a local department store. She told him she occupied the ground-floor flat with a woman friend, both of them single; they had worked together at the Town Hall until their retirement. Her friend was out shopping.

Lambert asked if she had known a David Hinckley who had rented the first-floor flat until some two and a half years ago.

'Oh yes,' she said with a smile. 'I remember him. He was the good-looking one, really rather stunning.'

'He had a flatmate?'

'He had two.' She could tell him their names: Preedy and Russell. 'Preedy was the one I knew best. I scarcely knew Hinckley at all, he was out a lot.'

He asked if she knew where Preedy and Russell were now.

'Russell's not in Cannonbridge any more,' she told him. 'He and Preedy both worked for that discount furniture place, the one that went bust.' This was a concern on the outskirts of Cannonbridge that had mushroomed into spectacular expansion a few years back and collapsed into equally spectacular bankruptcy twelve months ago. 'When the three of them left the flat here, Hinckley went to live out at Grayshott, and Russell and Preedy took a smaller flat not far from here. After the firm went bust Russell went off to London and found himself a job down there. Preedy's still living in Cannonbridge. He has a steady girlfriend here, a local girl, she lives at home with her parents. So of course he doesn't want to leave Cannonbridge, he keeps hoping things will pick up round here.'

'Can you give me his address?' Lambert asked.

'Yes, I can. He keeps in touch, he calls round to see if there's been any mail for any of them. Not that there ever is these days.' She smiled. 'Between you and me, I think he calls when the money's run out—I usually give him a good meal. Poor lad, he's living in a rather squalid bedsit on social security. He gets a few weeks' casual work now and then, but that's all.'

Lambert produced a couple of photographs and held them out. 'Do you recognize either of these girls?' he asked without preamble.

She glanced at the photographs and uttered a startled exclamation.

'It's those two girls,' she said in horror. She jerked her head back. 'You surely don't think any of those young men—'

'Did you ever see either of those girls here?' Lambert asked.

'Here? Certainly not.' She was appalled at the notion.

'You're positive?' He thrust Helen Mowbray's photograph at her. 'Did you never see her calling at the flat upstairs, when the three young men lived there?'

'No, never.' She looked up at him. 'But my friend and I only moved in here when we retired, that was a few months before the young men left.'

He held out Joanne's photograph. 'Do you know if she called at the upstairs flat recently, inquiring about her sister?'

'I certainly never saw her. The people upstairs never mentioned anyone calling like that. If she did call there during the day she'd have got no answer, she'd probably have come on down here and rung this bell. And if she'd called up there in the evening they wouldn't have been able to tell her anything, they never knew any of the three young men. They'd have sent her down to me, they know I keep in touch with Preedy.'

The street in which Preedy now lived was a good many steps down the social scale from the road Lambert had just left. An area of peeling, stucco-fronted houses let out in bedsits to students and the single unemployed; the front gardens concreted over, used as parking stands for old bangers.

Preedy's room was on the second floor. He was sitting at the table, reading, drinking coffee, eating a large, unwieldy sandwich, when Lambert knocked.

'Door's open,' he called out. Lambert turned the handle and went in. The room was small and dingy, poorly furnished; the air held lingering memories of many a fry-up.

Preedy glanced up at him in surprise, his mug of coffee halfway to his lips. A very thin young man, with a sharp, lean face.

Lambert told him who he was and the case on which he was working. Preedy continued to look up at him with the same startled gaze. Lambert added that he had just come from the flat, he had spoken to the woman on the ground floor.

Preedy roused himself. He set down his mug and waved a hand at the only other chair. 'Sit down,' he invited. 'Would you like some coffee?' Lambert shook his head. 'What do you want to see me about?' Preedy asked. 'I didn't know either of those girls.'

'David Hinckley was a friend of Helen Mowbray's,' Lambert said.

'David Hinckley?' Preedy echoed in astonishment.

'You didn't know that?'

'I certainly did not.'

Lambert produced his photographs. 'Did you ever see Helen at the flat?'

Preedy studied her face. 'No, never. Hinckley was hardly ever in the flat.'

'Did you know who his friends were?'

He shook his head. 'He didn't say where he was going or where he'd been, or who with. He wasn't a very chatty guy.'

'Are you still friendly with him?'

Preedy handed back the photographs. 'I never was all that friendly with him. Sharing the flat was just an arrangement that suited the three of us. I knew Russell slightly from work, we were never mates. He put up a notice in the canteen, looking for two other guys to share a flat. I went in with him. I was living in digs, I'd been thinking of branching out. The furniture warehouse was doing terrific business.' He grinned. 'We thought the good times were here at last. We couldn't find a third guy so Russell put an ad in the paper and Hinckley answered it. The three of us were in the flat getting on for two years. It worked OK, we never got in each other's way.' He had recovered sufficiently from his surprise to resume his attack on his sandwich. Judging from the fragments that dropped on to his plate, the filling consisted of chunks of cold fried potato laced with tomato ketchup.

'You don't see Hinckley these days?' Lambert asked.

'I see him all right, every now and then.' He grinned again. 'Swanning round Cannonbridge. But he doesn't see me, I've become invisible.' He waved his half-eaten sandwich. 'I suppose I might be the same if our positions were reversed.' He paused and frowned. 'No, I'm damned if I would. I could never be that po-faced.'

'When you were all living at the flat,' Lambert said, 'did you know about Hinckley's association with Mrs Wyatt?'

Preedy made a face. 'Never knew a thing. Nor did Russell. Never a breath of it. We didn't even guess when Hinckley told us he was leaving the flat to go and live out at Grayshott Manor. He said he was going there on a job, Mrs Wyatt was having a design studio built out there and he was to be in charge of it. He gave us the impression there was some sort of accommodation thrown in, a flat maybe. He was a pretty cagey type, never talked about himself.' He took another vast bite. 'Some time after we'd all left the flat, my girlfriend got talking one day to a woman who worked at Wyatt's, and she told her what the set-up was between Hinckley and Mrs Wyatt. That was the first we ever heard of it.'

No, Joanne Mowbray hadn't called at the bedsit, inquiring about Hinckley; Preedy had never had any contact with her.

'Was there ever a time at the flat when Hinckley appeared short of money?' Lambert asked. Preedy pondered but couldn't recall anything. 'He never asked either of you for a loan?' He shook his head. 'Did he say anything about an abortion? Having to pay the fees?'

'An abortion? You mean for Helen Mowbray?' His face expressed astonishment. 'No, he never said anything.'

'In general, did he seem flush or hard up?'

'He certainly never seemed short. But he didn't chuck it about. We shared the rent and rates between the three of us, the electricity and gas bills, all that sort of thing. Hinckley was always very careful about working out the exact figure, making sure he didn't pay a penny more than he should. Deeply devoted to money, I should say, our David.'

'Did he ever give the impression of being worried about something—something other than money?'

He pondered again. 'Not that I can recall. He wasn't an up-and-down sort of guy, he was always pretty much the same: quiet, not very forthcoming.'

'What sort of car did he drive?'

'He had an old Triumph Spitfire when he moved into the flat. Then about a year later he bought a brand new Alfa-sud—a beautiful car.'

'What happened to the Spitfire?'

'I asked him if he was trading it in but he said no, he knew someone who wanted it.'

'Did he mention who the someone was?'

'No.'

'Or if he was selling the car or making a present of it?'

'He didn't say.'

Preedy gave Lambert a long, thoughtful look. 'You don't think Hinckley had something to do with those two murders?'

'I don't think anything,' Lambert said. 'This is just the usual drill, following up every friendship, every relationship, right down to the most casual contact we get to hear about.'

He paused. 'Would the idea strike you as incredible?'

Preedy took another bite of his ragged confection. He chewed it slowly, washed it down with coffee. 'No,' he said at last. 'I can't honestly say it would strike me as totally incredible.'

It was after two when Lambert drove the Chief out to Blackshaw's. As they entered the car park Kelsey uttered an exclamation. 'There's Udell now!' Lambert halted the car and the Chief jumped out. Udell was sitting in his car some little distance away, about to pull out. At the sight of the Chief a look of irritated displeasure crossed his face. He switched off his engine and stepped out on to the tarmac. 'If you've ten minutes to spare,' the Chief said with iron affability. 'I know you're a busy man.'

Udell gave a loud sigh and looked at his watch. 'Ten minutes then,' he said grudgingly. 'I have an appointment.'

'We'll take a seat in your car,' Kelsey said with resolute good humour. He glanced back at Lambert and gave a little jerk of his head. Lambert got out of the car and came over.

'All right then,' Udell conceded with a bad grace. He got back into the driver's seat and Kelsey and Lambert got into the back. Udell half turned to face them, frowning, his lips jutting out in a way that seemed to indicate a minimal desire to be cooperative.

Kelsey got down to business without delay. 'You didn't mention that Helen Mowbray owned a car,' he said abruptly.

'Never occurred to me to mention it,' Udell answered at once, like a tennis player smartly returning a swift opening serve. 'If you'd asked me I'd have told you. The thought never crossed my mind. If I had remembered the car I'd have assumed you already knew about it. In any case it wouldn't have struck me as particularly important.' He sat looking alertly at the Chief, waiting for the next ball.

Kelsey banged it straight over the net. 'We're not mind-readers,' he said sharply. 'And we're not magicians. We have to have the information, all the information, never mind picking and choosing what folk think is important. Anything else that occurs to you, never mind how insignificant or trivial it may seem to you, you come along and tell us, pronto. We'll decide what's important and what's not important.'

Udell gave a sideways jerk of his head. 'Right you are,' he said with equal energy. 'Message received and understood.'

'What rent did you charge Helen Mowbray for the flat?' Kelsey went on without pause. Udell mentioned a weekly sum. Kelsey raised his eyebrows. 'That was certainly plenty.'

'It was what I'd been getting from the previous tenant,' Udell replied aggressively. 'Helen was very keen to have the flat, I wasn't at all keen to let it. I saw no reason to drop the price, I wasn't running a charitable home for working girls.'

'Did she ask you to drop the price?'

'She did not. She asked what the rent was. I told her, she agreed it. I wouldn't have taken less.' He jutted his lips out again.

'How did she pay the rent?'

'By the week. Normally it would have been by the month but it was a short let and I didn't know exactly how long she would be there, so I told her I wanted it by the week. She made no objection.'

'In what form was the payment made?'

'In cash.'

'Did you ask for cash?'

Udell's head came swiftly round. 'No. Why should I?'

Kelsey countered this question with another of his own. 'Were you surprised that she always paid in cash?'

He shrugged. 'I never gave it a thought. I had a number of properties, I was often paid in cash. It was all one to me.'

'Did you ever reduce the rent for her—after she moved in?'

He frowned. 'I did not. I told you, she said she could afford what I asked. That was the end of the matter.'

'Did you ever suggest reducing—or waiving—the rent?'

His frown deepened. 'I most certainly did not. Why on earth should I suggest such a thing?'

'In return for certain favours?'

'Favours?' Udell echoed. 'What kind of favours? Do you mean in return for secretarial work? When she did any work for me I paid her for it on exactly the same basis as I'd done before she moved into Holmwood.'

'No, I do not mean secretarial work,' Kelsey told him. 'I mean in return for more intimate favours.'

Udell's face glowed with anger. 'What kind of insinuation is that? Do you consider yourself entitled to make any kind of insulting insinuation you choose?'

'If you would just answer the question,' Kelsey said mildly.

He closed his eyes for a moment. 'No, I never suggested reducing or waiving the rent in return for favours of any kind, professional or personal. I neither asked for nor received any such favours. That is not and never has been the way I conduct business matters.'

'This work she did for you after she moved into Holmwood—was it to do with keeping two sets of books?' Udell's mouth jerked open. 'One set for the taxman,' Kelsey said, 'and another for yourself.'

'There were never two sets of books,' Udell responded with heat. 'There aren't now and never have been. The work she did for me was straightforward, run-of-the-mill secretarial and book-keeping work, the same sort of work she'd done for me all along.'

'Did you give her a gold bracelet as an additional payment for her work—or maybe by way of a present?'

'I certainly did not. I gave her no bracelet or any other kind of present.' Udell added suddenly in a tone of intense resentment, 'I never wanted to get mixed up in anything like this. You think you're doing someone a favour and this is what you get in return.'

'A favour?' Kelsey echoed.

'She begged and pleaded with me to let her have the flat.'

'Begged and pleaded?'

He pulled himself up short. 'That's probably putting it a bit strongly.' He attempted a laugh. 'She was pressing me, shall we say?'

'You're sure she didn't beg and plead?' Kelsey said. 'And you told her: OK, you can have the flat—on certain conditions. You knew the girl's unprotected situation, that she had no contact with her family.'

'I knew nothing about that,' Udell broke in. 'She never talked about anything like that.'

'Were you responsible for her pregnancy?' Kelsey suddenly fired at him.

Udell half rose to his feet, crouching in the confined space. 'You've gone too far! This is absolutely monstrous! I can't believe I'm obliged to sit here and take this kind of—'

'It would save us all a good deal of trouble,' Kelsey observed dispassionately, 'if you could refrain from exploding at every question and simply answer in a straightforward manner. The sooner you answer, the sooner you can get off to your appointment.'

Udell gave a smothered exclamation and glanced at his watch.

'In spite of what you may think,' Kelsey went on, 'I don't particularly enjoy putting this sort of question to you or anyone else. The nature of the investigation obliges me to put them. It also obliges you to answer them.'

Udell sank down again into his seat. He flashed the Chief a series of quick short glances and then appeared to take a grip on himself. 'No, I was not responsible for her pregnancy,' he said at last in a tight, fierce tone. 'I didn't know she was pregnant, I don't see why I should have known. I wasn't all that well acquainted with her, the only contact I had with her was by way of business.'

'Did she ask you for money to pay for an abortion?'

Udell visibly swallowed an angry response. 'She did not,' he said shortly.

'She had the abortion soon after you returned from Dorset—returned engaged to be married.'

'I told you, I know nothing about any abortion.'

'She was murdered shortly before you got married.'

'I know nothing about that either. Why do you keep connecting it all with me? With my engagement and marriage? What's any of it got to do with me?'

'Had Helen been trying to make trouble for you in connection with your forthcoming marriage?'

Udell glowered at him. 'In what way make trouble?'

'Threatening to tell your fiancée of your relationship?'

'There was no such relationship as the one you keep suggesting. There was no way she could possibly make trouble between me and Vera.'

'I put to you a sequence of events, a purely hypothetical sequence, you understand. Shortly after you came back from Dorset, engaged to be married, Helen told you she was pregnant. You gave her money for an abortion. When the time came for her to leave the flat she refused to play ball, she knew she had the whip hand, over your accounts as well as your marriage. She was demanding that you provide her with somewhere else to live, maybe a new car into the bargain. You could see no end to these demands, to the threat that would be permanently hanging over you, and over your marriage. So, to keep her quiet, you told her you agreed to her demands. You then disposed of her, went down to Dorset and got married.'

'There's not a word of truth in any of that from start to finish.' Udell sounded flat and weary, he was beginning to look pale and tired.

'Did you know of the existence of Stoneleigh? The derelict house where the bodies were found?'

'No, I did not know of it.' He was tense and rigid again, his glance once more sustained and unwavering.

'In the course of your activities as a property developer did you ever have occasion to visit the Stoneleigh area? To inspect the house and land?'

'I did not.'

'But you knew of the existence of the field?'

'I did not.' He fired off each denial in the same rapid tone.

'Not even as a location on the map?'

'Not even as that. Not in any way at all.'

'I find that hard to credit.'

By way of reply Udell merely raised his shoulders.

'Were you attracted to Helen?' Kelsey asked suddenly.

'No, I was not,' he answered with energy.

'She was generally considered a good-looking girl.'

He made an impatient gesture. 'I paid no attention to her looks.'

'Perhaps you're attracted to more mature women?'

'That's probably true,' Udell said after a moment, in a detached, dismissive tone.

Kelsey gave him a reflective stare. 'Odd, that. I should have thought, in view of that Tappenhall business, that your tastes lay in the opposite direction, that you were attracted by very young girls.'

As soon as the word Tappenhall fell on his ears Udell's face flushed bright crimson. He sat motionless and rigid. Lambert saw his fists clench. Then the colour ebbed, leaving his face deathly pale. 'Vera,' he said. 'My wife.' Sweat broke out on his brow. 'She knows nothing about any of that.' He looked at Kelsey with entreaty.

Kelsey jerked his head. 'I'm not in the business of telling women about their husbands' pasts,' he said brusquely. 'I ask you again: Did you find Helen attractive?'

Udell drew a little shuddering breath. 'Yes, I suppose so. But I didn't dwell on it.' He flashed at Kelsey a look of naked appeal, as of one human being to another. 'Do you imagine

I'd be fool enough to make another mistake like that Tappenhall business? It took me years to get over that. I'd built up a new life, I was thinking of getting married. Do you think I'd have thrown all that away? Do you think I'm incapable of learning a lesson? What kind of fool would I have to be—'

'The records of criminal history are full of precisely such fools.' Kelsey's words fell like stones and were followed by a silence. Udell sat unmoving, his face controlled now, wiped clear of expression.

'When Joanne Mowbray phoned you on the evening of Tuesday, March 1st,' Kelsey said, 'did you arrange to meet her on the following evening, telling her perhaps that you'd be making inquiries in the meantime about Helen, you thought you might have a lead?'

Udell shook his head slowly and wearily. 'No, I did not,' he said in a low voice. All the fire seemed to have gone out of him. 'You've got it all wrong,' he added. 'I had nothing to do with either of those girls. Not in the way you keep suggesting.'

'How did you spend that Wednesday evening? March 2nd. From, say, five o'clock until midnight.'

He took a diary from his pocket and turned the pages. 'I went out to see a couple of prospects,' he said after a minute or two. His tone grew firmer. 'People interested in having extensions built.'

'Do you usually call on prospects in the evening?'

'Yes, I often make calls in the evening or at weekends. It's a case of catching the husband at home, sometimes catching both of them, if the wife goes out to work as well.'

'What time were these appointments?'

'Seven-thirty and eight-thirty. I remember that evening clearly, I got orders from both those appointments, good orders—that doesn't happen every day. I came home for my tea as usual, that would be between half past five and six. Vera was there when I got home, she was in the house all

evening. I went out again at seven. I came home around ten
o'clock. I had a bite to eat and watched some TV. We went to
bed around eleven.'

'We'll have the names and addresses of those two
prospects,' Kelsey said. 'Then you can get off for your
appointment.'

Udell gave them the names. 'I'll have to go into the office
for the addresses,' he explained. 'I haven't got a note of them
here.'

'OK,' Kelsey said. 'Pop in and get them.'

Udell opened the car door. Half way out he paused and
glanced back at the Chief. 'I know you're only doing your
job,' he said on a hesitant, apologetic note. 'I shouldn't have
flown off the handle like that. Helen Mowbray—the kind of
relationship you suggested—I've never gone in for that kind
of thing, I've never been what you'd call a ladies' man.' He
looked away. 'That was part of the trouble, I suppose—the
old trouble, the Tappenhall business. I was always shy of
young women.' He attempted a grin. 'Still am, come to that.'
He gave Kelsey a level look. 'That's all over and done with, a
long time ago. I have a good marriage now, I set a very high
value on it, I wouldn't let anything spoil it.' He suddenly
ceased talking and darted off towards the office.

Kelsey got out of the car and walked across to a bay where
waste and refuse were neatly stowed, awaiting the arrival of a
contractor who called two or three times a week at the
factories on the estate. There were a great many flattened
cardboard boxes, a good deal of stout paper, polythene
wrappings, a sizeable quantity of tapes and cords, string and
twine.

And a number of large plastic bags, folded down. He stood
surveying the piles. Forensic hadn't been able to come up
with anything significant or distinctive in either the plastic
bags or the cord found at Stoneleigh; both were of an
everyday type and quality. Similar piles of packaging waste
could be found at many of the factories on the estate.

Nor was there any shortage of such materials at Wyatt Fashions.

Five minutes later Sergeant Lambert drove the Chief the half-mile to Fletcher's Plastics. 'Mr Fletcher's not in his office at the moment,' Mrs Ogilvie told them. 'He's somewhere in the works. I'll go and find him.'

Kelsey waved a hand. 'No need, you can probably tell us what we want to know. We're trying to trace a young woman we believe worked here a few years back. We don't know her maiden name but we believe she left here getting on for three years ago, to marry a farmer by the name of Stockman. We'd like her present address if you've got it.'

'I'm afraid that was before my time,' Mrs Ogilvie said, 'but Mr Ryland's sure to know. I'll go and get him.' As she reached the door she glanced out of the window and exclaimed, 'It's all right, Mr Ryland's in the yard, he's coming over here with Mr Fletcher.' A minute or two later the two men came in together, discussing with friendly animation some production detail.

'I'm sorry,' Fletcher said when he saw the Chief. 'I'd no idea you were here.'

'We've only just arrived,' Kelsey told him. He repeated his request for Mrs Stockman's address.

'No use asking me,' Fletcher said lightly. He jerked his head at Ryland. 'Better ask Jack here, he's your man. He remembers every female we've ever employed—and he'll tell you the colour of her eyes, into the bargain.'

Ryland grinned. 'Yes, sure I remember her, she was in the general office for five years. Competent girl, very punctual, wore glasses. Straight fair hair, cut in a fringe. Very good legs.' He grinned again. 'Her eyes were grey. I don't need to look up her address, I can give it to you.' He named a farm in a village twenty miles away.

'We could do with you in the Force,' Kelsey said. 'I'm much obliged.'

'If that's all, then,' Fletcher said, 'you won't mind if Jack gets off. He's standing in for me at a meeting at one of my other factories.' Kelsey gave a nod of acquiescence. 'You'd better take the Range Rover,' Fletcher told Ryland. 'There's still some water on that road.'

'Oh—while we're here,' Kelsey said suddenly, 'we'd better ask you both how you spent the evening of Wednesday, March 2nd. Routine, you understand, got to ask.'

'That was the day Joanne Mowbray phoned here, wasn't it?' Fletcher said. Kelsey inclined his head. 'Is that the last time anyone's heard of her?' Fletcher asked in a tone of lively curiosity. Kelsey didn't answer the question but merely repeated, 'If you could both tell us how you spent that evening. From, say, five o'clock until midnight.'

'Simple enough,' Fletcher observed. He took a diary from his pocket and glanced through it. 'I left the office with Jack here at half past five. I remember that, we were talking about Joanne's phone call as we left, Jack was asking me what she'd said. I went straight home. I spent the evening working on a speech with my wife—for a meeting on the Friday.'

'Did either you or your wife leave the house during the evening?'

'No. By the time we'd eaten and worked on the speech, it was time for bed.'

Kelsey glanced at Ryland. 'I can remember leaving here with Mr Fletcher, and talking about the phone call,' Ryland told him. 'I was trying to remember what I did after I got home. I'm afraid I don't keep a diary.' He looked down at the floor. 'I think that was the time I was decorating one of the bedrooms,' he said after a moment or two. 'Yes, that's right, I remember now. I spent every evening that week doing the bedroom—one of my wife's nieces was coming over to stay for a couple of days the following week.' He gave a decisive nod. 'Yes, that's it. I went straight home from here, had my tea and then got stuck into the decorating, I didn't go out again. It was the same drill every evening that week.'

'Was your wife in the house all the evening?'

Ryland's eyes roved the room. 'No, as a matter of fact she wasn't.' He gave a little laugh. 'I told her: There's no point in the two of us being stuck in the house, you might as well go out and enjoy yourself. She likes a game of darts, she's pretty hot stuff at it. She was out at the local pub, or one of the other pubs in town, every evening that week.' He laughed again. 'She'll remember that all right.'

'What time did she leave the house on the Wednesday evening?'

'She did the same every evening that week,' Ryland answered with an indulgent, amiable air. 'She gave me my tea and then went off. I washed up afterwards. That's the way we operate, because of the kids. We always pull together. If we can't both go out, we take it turn and turn about.' He waved a hand. 'Works very well. We've got four kids,' he added with pride. 'The oldest takes his O-levels this summer, the youngest is rising four. We've two girls in between, fifteen and nine.' He shook his head, smiling. 'They keep us pretty busy between them, I can tell you.' His grin showed signs of becoming fixed.

'What time did your wife get back from the pub that evening?' Kelsey asked.

'I suppose it would be around a quarter past, half past ten. I don't particularly recall the Wednesday evening, but that would be her usual time.'

Kelsey regarded him thoughtfully. 'Ever do any rough shooting?' he asked at last. Ryland looked surprised. Fletcher glanced sharply from Ryland to Kelsey and back again.

'I don't do much these days,' Ryland answered. 'I don't get the time. There's always plenty to keep me busy at home.'

'But you did a bit at one time?'

'A certain amount.'

'Did your shooting ever take you over Stoneleigh way?'

Lambert saw Mrs Ogilvie's mouth open in a little gasp.

'Difficult to remember after all this time just where we did go,' Ryland said lightly. 'We used to go about in a gang, half a dozen of us, old schoolmates.' He grinned again. 'You know how it is when you're young.' The expression on his face, his expansive gestures, his words, and the tone in which they were uttered, were all cheerful and relaxed. But the look in his eyes, anxious and unsmiling, seemed to belong to a different man.

CHAPTER 10

The Rylands lived on a modern housing development on the far side of the industrial estate, another mile and a half out from Cannonbridge. On this sunny afternoon of the school holidays Mrs Ryland was reclining at ease on the sofa in the sitting-room, with the curtains drawn against the sparkling sunshine. Her shoes were off, her feet up, her head rested against the cushions; she was absorbed in the latest episode of a television soap opera. The three older children had gone off about their own concerns, the youngest was playing with his collection of toy cars in a room across the hall. A box of chocolates lay open on a coffee table beside her; every now and then, without taking her eyes from the screen, she stretched out a hand and dipped into the box.

The drama had reached a particularly exciting point when Sergeant Lambert halted the car outside. She heard the ring of the doorbell but paid no attention. The bell rang a second and third time. She blew out a long breath of irritation, sat up and thrust her feet into her shoes. She levered herself up off the sofa and went along to the door.

'Yes?' She glanced out at the two men with barely suppressed hostility. By gum, Sergeant Lambert thought, she must have been a stunner once. He put her in her mid-thirties, running to fat. Her colouring was still striking: dark auburn hair, grey-green eyes with long dark lashes, a pale, creamy skin. But the corners of her mouth were chronically downturned, lines were already scoring her forehead, the flesh was beginning to pouch under the grey-green eyes.

Kelsey disclosed their identity and the case on which they were engaged. A frown appeared between her brows. 'It's Jack you're wanting to talk to,' she told him brusquely. 'He's never at home this time of the afternoon, he's at work.'

'If we could just step inside for a moment,' Kelsey said.

Her frown deepened. 'It's no use talking to me. I can't tell you anything about those Mowbray girls. I never go near Fletcher's. I've no more idea who was employed there or what goes on down there than the man in the moon.'

'One or two little points you might be able to help us with,' Kelsey said. 'But I'm not sure it's a good idea to conduct our business on the doorstep.' He glanced at the nearby houses.

'I've nothing to hide from the neighbours,' she declared in a loud, challenging voice.

There was a rush of childish feet along the hall behind her and a little boy, three or four years old, came running up to her, holding out a toy car. 'I can't make it go,' he called out as he came, in a tone of whining complaint. At the sight of the two strangers he came to an abrupt halt and stuck a finger in his mouth.

'I suppose you'd better come along inside,' Mrs Ryland said ungraciously to the two men. The boy held the car up to her, shaking it impatiently. 'I can't make it go,' he said again.

'Oh do stop whingeing,' she told him sharply. She stood scowling at him. The child looked as if he would burst into tears.

Lambert reached down and gently took the toy from the child's fingers. 'You rub the back wheels on the floor, like this.' He crouched to demonstrate. He released the car which instantly sped off along the hall. The child gave a whoop of delight and ran after it.

'We won't keep you many minutes,' the Chief told Mrs

Ryland as Lambert closed the front door. 'We know how busy you must be.'

She gave a grunt of reluctant acquiescence and led the way into the darkened sitting-room. She crossed to the television set and switched off the sound but she didn't trouble to draw back the curtains. She sank down on to the sofa but the two men remained standing. After a moment she told them grudgingly, 'I suppose you'd better sit down, seeing you're here.' They took their seats in easy chairs on either side of the hearth. 'Get a move on then,' she urged. 'What is it you want to ask me?'

'Just a matter of routine checking,' Kelsey said. 'I realize how irritating it must be for you, being disturbed when you're trying to snatch a few minutes to yourself, but I assure you you're not the only one, we're doing the same thing all over the town. We have to check everyone's movements, everyone connected in any way at all with the case, however, slightly. They none of them like it, any more than you do, I can promise you. We don't relish getting across folk, I'm sure you appreciate that, but it's regulations, we have to do it, there'd be hell to pay if we didn't.'

'Yes, I suppose so,' she said, her manner a shade less hostile. 'I suppose you've got to do your duty.'

'That's exactly it!' he exclaimed as if she had made an observation of profound significance. 'If only everyone was as understanding as you. Now Mr Ryland—and of course Mr Fletcher too—they've both told us what their movements were on the evening of March 2nd. But we have to check everything, we can't make any exceptions. We'll be checking with Mrs Fletcher as well.'

'What's so special about March 2nd?' she asked suddenly, unable to repress curiosity.

'I'm afraid I can't answer that,' he replied in tones of deep regret. 'Regulations again, we're not allowed to. So there we are—I have to ask you if you can recall exactly how your husband spent that evening.'

She looked down at the carpet, then she raised her head and asked, 'What did Jack tell you he was doing that evening?'

Kelsey gave a little shake of his head. 'There again, we're not allowed to answer that. What each person tells us is said in the strictest confidence. Got to be, otherwise no one would ever tell us anything at all. We won't disclose to anyone, not even to your husband, anything you tell us, and of course the same goes for him.'

There was another pause. 'The first Wednesday in March,' he said encouragingly. 'That might help you to remember.'

She sat turning her head this way and that, frowning. 'I can't remember anything special,' she said after a minute or two. She relapsed into silence. When it began to look as if she was prepared to sit there for the rest of the afternoon without opening her mouth again, he asked, 'Does your husband perhaps go in for do-it-yourself? Does that ring a bell?'

'Oh yes,' she said at once, 'he's always got some job or other on the go. He's retiling the bathroom just now.'

'Has he done any decorating lately?' he was forced to ask when she showed no signs of adding anything further.

She pondered. 'The last job he did was one of the bed-rooms.'

'Can you remember exactly when that was?'

She pondered again. 'I know it took him several days. 'He never will hurry, he always has to do the job properly.' She looked up at Kelsey. 'I suppose it could have been about that time, the beginning of March.' She paused. 'Yes, that's right—my niece came over for a couple of nights, that's why he did the bedroom. That was early in March.'

'Do you go out much in the evenings?' Kelsey asked with a casual air.

She gave a little snorting laugh. 'I go out as often as I get the chance.'

'Do you get down to the pub at all? Do you like a game of darts?'

'I certainly do,' she answered with energy. 'I was a dab hand with a dart at one time. I was in the ladies' team at the Coach and Horses. We won all the cups one year.'

'Can you remember if you got out much in the evenings around that time, early March?'

She looked at him reflectively. In the shadowy half light he saw calculation move across her face. 'I believe I did.' Her tone grew firmer. 'Yes, that's right, I was out that evening you mentioned, that Wednesday.'

'Did you get out every evening that week?'

She didn't answer for several seconds, then she said, 'Yes, now I come to think of it, I believe I did get out most evenings that week.' She stared at Kelsey, her eyes wide and wary. 'It might even have been every evening. Yes, I think it was. Jack was busy with the decorating, he was here to keep an eye on the kids.'

'Total waste of time, that was,' Kelsey observed sourly to Lambert as they walked out through the front gate a few minutes later. 'All she's concerned with is saying whatever she thinks will square with what she fancies her precious husband has already told us.' He glanced at his watch as they reached the car. 'Stop at the next phone box. We'll give Mrs Stockman a ring, see if we can get over there now and have a word with her.'

In the short time she had been married—three years in June—Mrs Stockman had created for herself a full and varied life, in the local community as well as on her husband's farm. When Kelsey phoned he caught her as she was about to leave for a committee meeting in the village hall, in connection with a Whitsun pageant to celebrate the quatercentenary of the village church. 'If you can get over here by a quarter to four,' she told him, 'I'll make a point of being back by then.'

And true to her word, as Sergeant Lambert turned the car into the big square courtyard at the rear of the farmhouse, Mrs Stockman drove up from the direction of the village. She pulled up behind them and jumped out of her car. A slim, neat-looking young woman, twenty-eight or thirty, with lively eyes and a fresh country complexion. She still wore spectacles, elegantly framed. Her fair hair was no longer cut in a fringe but was curled becomingly back from her face. Ryland had certainly been right about her legs, Lambert noted; they were remarkably good. And her eyes were grey.

'An appalling business about poor Helen Mowbray,' she said as she took them in through the back door of the farmhouse into a cool, dim rear hall furnished with massive pieces of ancient oak. 'I couldn't believe it when I read it in the paper. I didn't know her sister, of course—I didn't even know she had a sister.' Joanne had made no kind of contact with her.

She led the way into a large old kitchen cosy from the warmth of an all-night stove. She lifted one of the hotplate covers and drew forward a kettle from the back of the stove; it came to the boil almost at once.

'Helen never talked about her family,' she said as she reached down cups from a dresser.

'How well did you know her?' Kelsey asked.

'Not very well. I always felt a little sorry for her, she seemed very much alone. We sometimes had coffee together at break, when we were both at Fletcher's. Once or twice we went for lunch together.' She smiled. 'It was mostly me that did the talking. I was always full of plans for the wedding, and she seemed happy enough to listen.'

She made the tea and brought a freshly-baked chocolate cake from the larder. 'Did you keep up with her after she left Fletcher's?' Kelsey asked as she cut him a slice.

'Not really. I was always so busy. The only time I saw her again was when she came to the wedding, and I didn't get much of a chance to talk to her then.'

Kelsey asked if she knew of any men friends of Helen's. She shook her head. 'I can't remember her mentioning anyone.'

'She wasn't friendly with any man who worked at Fletcher's?'

'Not that I ever saw.' She paused and then added on a hesitant note, 'I take it you met Jack Ryland at Fletcher's?'

'Yes, we've met him,' Kelsey said. 'Was she friendly with him?'

Again she hesitated. 'I can't really say that she was. He was in the office a lot, of course. She was always pleasant, always polite to him.' She moved a hand. 'Perhaps I ought not to say this but it's just—the kind of man he is.'

'What kind of man is that?'

'His nickname in the office is Randy Jack, that'll give you the general idea. I used to live in the same street as his wife when we were both children. My elder sister went to school with her. My parents still live in the same street and so does Mrs Ryland's mother—her father died some years ago. My mother often has a chinwag with Mrs Ryland's mother. Mrs Ryland was a very pretty girl, really very striking-looking. She was the only girl in the family, her father spoiled her terribly.' She drank her tea. 'Ryland had to marry her when she was sixteen, she got pregnant.'

'He didn't want to marry her?'

'He certainly did not, he didn't want to marry anyone. He was only twenty or twenty-one, he had half a dozen girls on a string, he was probably looking forward to years of playing the field. But she had a father and five brothers, and they'd made up their mind Jack was going to marry her. Jack always fancied himself as a pretty hard nut but he was no match for that lot, tough wasn't the word for them.' She smiled. 'I don't think he felt he had a great deal of option over the marriage. Of course all this was before they handed out abortions the way they do now.'

'Did you know Helen Mowbray had an abortion?' Kelsey asked her.

She set down her cup with a clatter. 'Never!' She stared at him in astonishment. 'When was that?' Kelsey didn't answer and after a moment she let it go. 'Ryland always has some girl in the office,' she told him. 'His tastes don't seem to have altered over the years, he still likes them young and green—and willing.'

'Doesn't sound much like Helen Mowbray.'

She looked earnestly up at him. 'I really have no reason to suppose there ever was anything between them. It was just—she was such a good-looking girl, and she never talked about any men friends. It crossed my mind once or twice, maybe she and Ryland had something going.' She shook her head slowly. 'She was a very close-mouthed girl, she'd have been perfectly capable of keeping it quiet from the rest of us.'

'Does Mrs Ryland know about these girls?'

'She knows all right. She left him over it once, five or six years ago. She flounced out of the house and took herself off back home. Her father was dead by then and her brothers had all married and left home, so it was just her mother.' She smiled. 'Her mother had turned into a real merry widow, she was having the time of her life—still is, from what my mother tells me. Old-time dancing and whist drives, coach trips and church socials, she was fairly revelling in it after all the years she'd spent bringing up a big family. She wasn't best pleased when her daughter came marching in again with three kids.

'She kept telling her she ought to make it up with Jack, what did it matter if he strayed now and then, it was her he really loved, and so on and so forth. And of course the kids missed their Dad and they played their mother up. Jack's the one that keeps them in order, they've always been able to run rings round her.' She stood up and began to clear away the tea-things. 'And she'd never before had to live in a household where there wasn't a man to fetch and carry for her, do all the odd jobs, run her about in a car—she's never learned to drive.'

She pulled on a pair of rubber gloves and ran hot water

into the sink. 'She stayed a couple of months with her mother, it was more than enough for both of them. Jack kept going round there, asking her to go back home. He's not the sort that would ever want a divorce, he'd never want to marry one of his girls, he's far too fond of his children, he'd never want to lose them. And his wife's the last person that could manage on her own in a single-parent set-up. I couldn't see any other man taking her on with the children. She's nowhere near as good-looking as she used to be, and she's never been noted for a sweet temper.'

She began to wash up the tea-things. 'She and Jack were living in a small, old-fashioned house when she marched out. She saw her chance and made Jack promise to move them into a larger, modern house, if she went back to him. He was delighted, he'd have promised anything, so of course she went back.'

She shook her head. 'In no time at all she was pregnant again. But they seem to rub along all right now. He keeps his goings-on as discreet as possible and she keeps her eyes tight shut.'

'How long has Ryland worked at Fletcher's?' Kelsey asked.

'Ever since the factory opened, that would be about nine years ago now. He had half a dozen different jobs before that, he never seemed to settle, never amounted to much. Fletcher took him on as a factory hand but he soon moved up from that.'

She replaced the crockery on the dresser. 'Jack's good at his job, he's efficient and reliable. He's made himself very useful to Fletcher. He's pretty good at the contract side, he has a good head for business, he can drive a shrewd bargain. If Fletcher puts him in charge of something, Fletcher can forget it—and that's something Fletcher certainly appreciates. With all his other businesses and his political interests, it's a big thing to Fletcher to be able to delegate with an easy mind.' She smiled. 'If there's one thing that makes Fletcher hopping mad, it's having to chase round after someone, seeing they've done what he told them to.' She hung up her rubber gloves. 'It was a lucky day for Jack Ryland when he walked in through the gates of Fletcher's Plastics—and, to be fair, I don't think it was a bad day for Fletcher, either.'

Kelsey stood up to leave. 'Does Fletcher know about Ryland's goings-on?'

She pondered. 'I never saw any sign that Fletcher was aware of them. He doesn't concern himself with the running of the office, he leaves all that to Jack. Even if he did know, I don't think it would bother him, he'd trust Jack not to do anything that would interfere with the smooth running of the place. Fletcher would put his foot down pretty smartly if there was any question of that.'

As Lambert drove the car out into the lane he said, 'I very much doubt that Ryland did leave the office that Wednesday at the same time as Fletcher. If Ryland was up to some of his hanky-panky with one of the girls, he'd have got the wind up after the murder investigation began, for fear his little capers might come out. He might easily have asked Fletcher if he'd mind saying they left together. Fletcher would probably go along with that, he'd see no real harm in it. He wouldn't want to drop Ryland in it at home, over a bit of slap and tickle.'

Kelsey gave a grunt. 'Could be. But it could also be that Ryland told Fletcher he was with one of the girls that evening, but the truth of the matter might have been that he was dealing with Joanne Mowbray.' He thrust out his lips. 'Fletcher appears to trust Ryland a lot, too much, possibly. Suppose Ryland's been getting his sticky fingers into the till over the years, and suppose he was doing it at one time with Helen Mowbray's assistance, passing some of the proceeds her way. The Helen gets pregnant and Ryland takes fright, he tries to break off the association. But Helen won't let go, she starts to make threatening noises—so he gets rid of her.' He passed a hand across his jaw. 'That redhead in the office,

I'll bet she's Ryland's current fancy.' He glanced at his watch. 'We'll catch her as she comes out of work.'

They had been sitting watching the front gates at Fletcher's for the best part of ten minutes, the homegoing cars and bicycles had diminished to a thin trickle. 'There she is!' Lambert suddenly exclaimed. Two girls came round the side of one of the buildings, the younger one talking with animation, her gold-auburn hair gleaming in the late sunlight. When they reached the gates they halted for a moment, chatting and laughing, then they separated. The redhead walked away to her right along the main road, in the direction of Cannonbridge.

Lambert slid the car out and followed discreetly in her wake. Thirty or forty yards along the road she crossed over and went down a side street. She didn't look round but kept steadily on. She was smartly dressed with a pretty, rounded figure; she held herself well, walked with a confident air.

When she drew level with a long, high, garden wall, Lambert drew up beside her and halted. She slackened her pace and turned her head to glance at them. Kelsey stepped out on to the pavement. She knew him at once. Her face took on a mulish look, wary, tinged with apprehension.

'Hello, Sharon,' Kelsey greeted her, plucking a name from the air.

She shook her head and smiled, with an air of relief. 'You've got the wrong girl,' she informed him. 'My name's Debbie.'

'Yes, of course, Debbie,' he replied amiably. Her smile vanished. She stood looking at him in silence. Her full, ripe mouth had a lingering look of childhood.

'One or two questions we'd like to ask you,' Kelsey told her. 'You can sit in the car while we chat. It won't take more than a couple of minutes.'

She gave him a challenging stare. 'You can't make me get in. I've done nothing wrong. I know my rights.'

'Perhaps you also know your duties.' His tone was a shade less amiable. 'One of them is to assist the police in the course of an investigation.' Her jaw hardened, she made no move. 'I can offer you a choice,' he added. 'You can either get in the car now and answer come questions, or we can call in at your home and ask our questions there, in front of your parents.'

She offered no further argument. She made an angry gesture but stooped and got into a rear seat. Kelsey got in beside her. She pressed right up into the corner, as far away from him as possible.

'You have a boyfriend?' he asked.

She stared ahead. 'I've got lots of boyfriends.'

'You like older men?'

She turned her head and gave him a bold, appraising look. 'Are you propositioning me?'

'Cut out the gags,' he told her sharply. 'Answer the question.'

'I like some older men,' she answered with a movement of her shoulders.

'What time did you leave work on Wednesday, March 2nd?'

She stared ahead again. 'The usual time, I suppose.'

'Did you leave by yourself or with someone else?'

'I can't remember that now. It's weeks ago.'

'You remember all right. Which was it?'

She said nothing but set her jaw.

'You're friendly with Mr Ryland,' Kelsey said.

'What of it? I'm friendly with a lot of folk from work.'

'On the evening of Wednesday March 2nd you did one of two things. Either you stayed behind with Ryland or else he picked you up in his car after you left Fletcher's and the pair of you drove off somewhere for an hour or two.' She made no reply. 'Which was it?' he demanded.

'I did neither of those things,' she exclaimed angrily. 'I went straight home from work.'

'But you are playing around with Ryland?'

She set her mouth in a mutinous line. 'If you're asked that in court,' he added, 'you'll have to answer. Or end up in gaol.'

She flashed him a fierce glance. 'He hasn't done anything,' she declared with force. 'He has nothing to do with your case. What does it matter to you if we—' She broke off. 'What he was doing that evening, it had nothing to do with those two girls.'

'I'm not saying it has,' Kelsey said in a voice of sweet reason. 'But we have to ask a lot of questions about folk who're only on the fringe of the inquiry, it's the same in every murder case. We have to get the whole picture of what happened that evening. Every little detail is important.'

'It's my Dad,' she said abruptly. 'He'd skin me alive—' She fell silent again.

'Two girls murdered,' Kelsey said. 'Strangled with lengths of cord. Can you imagine a death like that? One of the girls about your age, all her life before her. A good, decent girl. Probably never harmed a living creature since the day she was born.'

She put a hand up to her forehead, she lowered her head, shielding her eyes with her outspread fingers. Kelsey let her remain in silence. After a minute or two she appeared to reach a decision. She raised her head and gave him a direct, steady look. 'You can't take me to court, I've done nothing against the law. You've no grounds for charging me with anything.' She reached for the door handle. 'Those two girls are dead, there's nothing I can tell you that can bring them back. But I'm alive, I've got my Dad to reckon with.' She opened the door and stepped boldly out. She walked rapidly away up the street.

Kelsey sat looking after her, frowning. 'Better get back to the station,' he instructed Lambert. He gave a gigantic yawn. No point in calling in at Fletcher's home later on this evening, he had seen the posters advertising one of Fletcher's ward meetings. 'Tomorrow,' he told Lambert as the car moved off. 'We'll call in on Fletcher at home tomorrow morning, see if we can get him to shift from his story about the time Ryland left the office that evening.'

Some five hours later, as the Chief lay stretched out in bed, on the point of dropping into a pole-axed sleep, his eyes jerked open on a sudden disquieting thought: The police investigation had clearly followed the same lines as Joanne's search for her sister—but was it not possible that Joanne had managed to pursue the trail somewhat further, had succeeded in reaching some person they hadn't so far encountered, of whose existence they had as yet not the slightest suspicion?

CHAPTER 11

Shortly after ten on Saturday morning Lambert drove in through the handsome wrought-iron gates of Pearmain House, nine miles to the south-east of Cannonbridge. The paintwork of the gates had recently been renewed, the gilded tips of the long black spears glittered in the sunshine. He ran the car up the drive—immaculate surface, free from weeds—and halted by the front door. A fine Queen Anne house in rosy, mellowed brick, a graceful portico at the head of a flight of semi-circular steps.

Lambert pressed the bell. Kelsey stepped back and looked up at the elegant face of the house; he glanced about at the disciplined lawns, the orderly flowerbeds, the shrubbery brilliant with berberis, camellia, rhododendron.

Footsteps sounded on the gravel and an old man—a gardener, by the look of him—came round the side of the house. White-haired and stoop-shouldered, pale blue eyes, a tanned and wrinkled skin.

'There's no one at home,' he called out as he came.

'They've gone off to the races with Mr Woodroff, Mrs Fletcher's father. They won't be back till late.'

'No matter,' Kelsey told him. 'We'll catch them another time. Wouldn't mind a day at the races myself,' he added jovially.

'Nor me,' the gardener declared. 'Very fond of horses, always have been. A place I worked at in my younger days, they used to keep horses. The lady and her daughters went riding every morning, hail, rain or shine. Mrs Fletcher now, she's not all that keen. She likes the day out and all that, but it might just as well be motor-car racing as far as she's concerned. Now Mr Fletcher—' he moved his head in approval—'he really enjoys his day at the races. He knows a bit about horses too. Brought up with them as a lad, he told me. His grandfather used to breed horses.'

'Somewhere in these parts, that would be?' Kelsey asked idly.

'No, not round here, down in Devon. Or was it Cornwall? One of those places anyway, somewhere down in the South-West. Lovely part, the South-West. That's right, now I come to think of it, I believe it was Devon. Old family place, something-or-other Hall.' He pondered. 'He did mention the name once when we were having a chat. Used to be Master of Foxhounds, his grandfather, local squire, you know the sort of thing.' He suddenly jabbed at the air with a couple of fingers. 'Ebrington Hall, that was it.'

'We'll have to come back tomorrow morning,' Kelsey said to Lambert as they got back into the car.

'Sunday tomorrow,' Lambert reminded him. 'Will Fletcher like that?'

Kelsey snorted. 'He can like it or lump it. We don't run the Force to suit Preston Fletcher.'

Sunday morning was clear and bright. At ten o'clock Sergeant Lambert once again drove up to the front door of Pearmain House. Two cars stood in the driveway: a Daimler

Sovereign, biscuit-coloured, three years old, and a green Range-Rover, last year's registration. Lambert paused briefly to glance at the Daimler with an appreciative eye.

Fletcher's wife, Veronica, answered their ring at the door. In her early thirties, tall and straight-backed, with a long-boned, angular figure. She wore expensive casual clothes; her brown hair, long and thick, was elegantly looped up on top of her head. Her face was neither beautiful nor plain, the kind of face that looks out of every photograph of Speech Day at a nobby girls' school: good breeding, good habits inculcated early, good food from birth, good doctors, good dentists, good hairdressers.

She said nothing but gave them an authoritative, questioning look. Kelsey disclosed his identity and asked if he might speak to her husband.

'He's busy just now,' she informed him on a note of rebuke. She had a high, assured voice. 'He's with my father.' As if that must be enough to dismiss any intrusion. When Kelsey remained unmoving on the step she added with a trace of impatience,' 'They're discussing the local election campaign. They won't want to be disturbed.'

'We won't keep him long,' Kelsey assured her.

She gave him a glance of keen appraisal. 'Very well, then.' She stepped back and held the door wide for them to enter. She led the way along the hall and opened a door on the left.

'It's Chief Inspector Kelsey and Sergeant Lambert,' she announced as she went in. Kelsey followed her into the room without waiting for an invitation.

Preston Fletcher and his father-in-law were seated together on a sofa before a long coffee table spread with papers. Fletcher held a clipboard in one hand and a pen in the other. He glanced up as they came in.

'I don't know if you've met my father,' Mrs Fletcher said. Kelsey acknowledged the introduction. He knew Woodroff by sight and reputation. Very tall, with a spare, bony frame;

a shrewd, strongly modelled face, dark bushy eyebrows, a head of iron-grey hair, still thick and wavy. He came from a highly respected county family, had managed the family wine-importing business until his retirement seven or eight years ago; he had long been a widower.

'Sunday morning,' Woodroff observed in a tone that just stopped short of outright discourtesy. 'Is this the time you normally choose to go about your business?'

Kelsey ignored the question. 'We'd like to confirm one or two details,' he told Fletcher.

'A time and place,' Woodroff interjected. 'A man is surely entitled to peace ad quiet in his own home on a Sunday morning.'

Fletcher gave the Chief a glance tinged with amusement. 'Perhaps you could call in at the office tomorrow morning,' he suggested amiably. He nodded at the papers on the coffee table. 'We are rather busy just now.'

Kelsey remained where he was. 'I'm sorry to have disturbed you,' he said, 'but now that we are here, perhaps I could ask you if you're absolutely certain about the time you and Mr Ryland left the office on the evening of Wednesday, March 2nd.'

'Yes, of course,' Fletcher answered readily. 'We left at five-thirty. No doubt about it.'

'A trivial detail like that,' Woodroff said loudly. 'Surely it could have waited till the morning.' Fletcher half-smiled at Kelsey.

'Preston got home at the usual time,' Mrs Fletcher told the Chief. 'I looked it up in my diary after he told me you'd been asking about it. Neither of us went out anywhere that evening. We spent the whole of that evening and the next working on the speech for Friday.'

'Thank you,' Kelsey said. 'I'm much obliged.' He looked at Fletcher. 'You're quite certain that Mr Ryland left at the same time as yourself?'

'Quite certain,' Fletcher answered without hesitation. 'I

can clearly remember talking to him about the phone call from Joanne Mowbray as we crossed the yard.'

'You definitely saw him get into his car and drive off?' Kelsey persisted. 'You're certain he didn't go back into the office?' Woodroff uttered a sound of lively exasperation.

'I don't know that I could actually swear I saw Jack drive off,' Fletcher said after a couple of moments, 'but I'm positive I saw him get into his car. I didn't see him go back into the office, I'm quite sure of that.' He frowned. 'What's all this in aid of?'

Kelsey didn't answer that. He asked, 'Then you can't say what direction Mr Ryland took after driving out of the car park?'

'No, I can't,' Fletcher said shortly. He slapped his clipboard down on the coffee table.

'Is it possible—' Kelsey began but Fletcher interrupted him. 'I don't know that I care to continue this conversation. If you've any more questions along the same lines, I suggest it's Ryland you should be asking, not me.'

'And at a more civilized time,' Woodroff put in. He leaned forward and picked up a sheaf of papers. 'Perhaps we might now be allowed to get on with what I came over here this morning especially to do.' He shafted a single piercing glance at Kelsey. 'And while you're in the process of gathering information, it might interest you to learn that I've more than a passing acquaintance with the Chief Constable.'

'Right then,' Kelsey said to Lambert between his teeth as he got into the car again. 'We'll trot along to Fletcher's office tomorrow morning, if that's what they want. We'll go after the funeral. We'll ask the same questions again, we'll keep on asking them until they're answered.'

Lambert started the engine and the Chief stared gloomily ahead. 'The devil of it is,' he said, 'Woodroff might very well have a word with the Chief Constable. They play golf together.' It would make no difference to what he proposed to do, only to the openness with which he did it. As the car

moved off down the drive he thumped a fist into his palm.
'The hell with it. Won't be the first black mark I've had. I
very much doubt it'll be the last.'

The funeral of Helen and Joanne Mowbray took place at
ten-thirty on Monday morning. Arnold Lockyear had decided on cremation and the nearest crematorium was in a
much larger town fifteen miles the other side of Martleigh,
the best part of forty miles from Cannonbridge. As a con-
sequence there were very few sightseers and curiosity-
mongers in the little chapel attached to the crematorium.

The ceremony was brief and sombre. Arnold Lockyear
looked pale and ill at ease. He kept his head lowered throughout. There were no relatives apart from Lockyear; no neighbours, apart from Mrs Snape. She had brought with her
three girls who had been in the same class at school as Joanne
Mowbray, and she had also arranged for a large and showy
wreath, subscribed for, according to the legend on the card,
by Friends and Neighbours from Thirlstane Street.

The rest of the congregation consisted mainly of reporters,
photographers and policemen. There were flowers from the
school the girls had attended, from both the Cannonbridge
agencies for which Helen had worked, and from Mrs
Huband and Miss Gallimore, though neither landlady
attended the funeral. There was nothing from David
Hinckley, nothing from Vincent Udell, nothing from
Wyatt Fashions, nothing from any member of the firm of
J. Preston Fletcher.

Immediately after the funeral Sergeant Lambert drove the
Chief back to Cannonbridge. They went straight out to the
industrial estate; it was by now almost half past twelve.

If the Chief was expecting a cool reception after his
intrusion into the Sabbath peace of Pearmain House he was
agreeably surprised. Fletcher greeted him with a smile. 'No
fobbing you off, is there?' he said amiably as he took the two
men into his office. 'You'd make a good salesman, Chief

Inspector. I hope you didn't mind my father-in-law yester-day. He's inclined to get a bit aërated at times.'

Kelsey merely inclined his head by way of reply. 'I'd like to speak to yourself and Mr Ryland together,' he said. 'I won't take up any more of your time than I can help.'

'I'm afraid Ryland's out at the moment,' Fletcher told him as he brought forward a couple of chairs. 'But he should be back any minute.'

Kelsey sat down. He made no attempt at conversation but disposed himself patiently to wait. After a minute or two Fletcher said in an easy, friendly tone, 'Look here, Chief Inspector, what is all this about? You surely can't for one moment imagine that Jack Ryland had anything to do with those two murders?'

'We're not in the business of imagining who might or might not have had anything to do with the murders,' Kelsey replied with the air of a man who has made the same observation—couched in varying terms—more times than he has blacked his boots. 'We're trying to account for the whereabouts of everyone even remotely connected with the case. We can't make any exceptions.' He levelled a glance at Fletcher. 'And we can't exempt anyone simply because someone else chooses to make a fuss about it.'

'I grant you all that,' Fletcher said with an air of great reasonableness and good humour, 'but to my certain knowl-edge you've already checked Ryland's movements twice. Yet here you sit once again, apparently determined to check them a third time. I very much doubt you're treating the rest of the local population in the same way.' He looked at Kelsey, inviting a response, but the Chief said nothing. Fletcher gave a resigned sigh and glanced at his watch. 'He can't be much longer,' he said in an ordinary business tone. He pulled open a drawer of his desk and took out an unopened packet of mints. He tore off the end of the green and white wrapper and held the packet out to the Chief.

Kelsey felt the hairs stiffen along the back of his scalp. He sat rigid for a moment, then he leaned forward and took the packet from Fletcher. He removed a mint and handed the packet back. Fletcher offered the mints to Lambert who took one and put it in his mouth. Kelsey suddenly pushed back his chair and stood up.

'We can't wait any longer,' he said. 'We must get back to the station.' Lambert glanced at him in surprise.

Fletcher got to his feet. 'Admit it,' he said to Kelsey with a grin. 'You've changed your mind about Ryland, you know you're barking up the wrong tree.' Kelsey didn't return his grin.

They left the office and walked across to the car. Kelsey got in beside Lambert. He leaned back and closed his eyes.

'It was Fletcher,' he said as the car moved out. 'Fletcher killed Joanne. And Helen. Fletcher killed them both.' He had a terrible desire to weep.

'Fletcher?' Lambert echoed in a voice of total incredulity.

Kelsey opened his eyes and sat up. He sprang open his right fist, disclosing the mint and a fragment of tinfoil, a scrap of green and white paper. Lambert glanced down at them.

'In the right-hand pocket of Joanne Mowbray's anorak,' Kelsey said. 'A piece of green and white paper and a scrap of tinfoil, screwed up together. Torn from a packet of mints. The brand of mints Fletcher uses.'

CHAPTER 12

'Is that all?' Lambert asked in astonishment. 'Thousands of people buy those mints. I buy them myself.'

The Chief took an envelope from an inside pocket and put the mint and the scraps of paper and tinfoil carefully inside. 'Joanne was in Fletcher's office that Wednesday evening,' he said with certainty. 'She sat opposite him, across the desk.'

He put the envelope in his pocket. 'It must have been a hell of a shock for Fletcher when he got back to the office that Monday afternoon, and Mrs Ogilvie told him Helen Mowbray's sister had been in, asking questions. Until that moment he probably didn't know Joanne existed.' He stared out through the windscreen. 'When he spoke to her over the phone on the Wednesday afternoon, she could have said something that told him she was getting dangerously close to the truth.'

He struck his fists together. 'He tells her he may have a lead about Helen but he's very busy just now, he has a customer waiting. If she'll call in later, say about six, he'll be free then to talk to her.

'At five-thirty he makes a point of leaving the office with Ryland. He gets into his car and starts it up. As soon as Ryland drives off, Fletcher gets out of his car again. When Joanne shows up he tells her any load of codswallop that will serve his purpose—he's heard of someone who may know where Helen is, he'll be glad to run her over there now— anything that will persuade Joanne to get into his car and sit happily beside him. Joanne is overjoyed, she offers no objection. She gets into the car and they drive off. At some suitable spot Fletcher stops the car.'

'He'd have been late home,' Lambert pointed out. 'His wife says he came home at the usual time.'

Kelsey dismissed that with a wave of his hand. 'He phoned his wife before Joanne arrived, he told her he had a tricky deal on, he'd be late home. Afterwards, when we start asking questions, he tells his wife he doesn't want to tell us where he was that evening, it could be a bit dicey, he'd rather not be too specific about that business deal, it wouldn't do for it to come out just before the council elections. Better say he got home as usual. She'd agree to that. Why wouldn't she?'

'And Ryland?'

'I don't believe Ryland knows anything about the murders, I don't think he has any suspicion of Fletcher. He's

quite sure Fletcher drove off home at five-thirty, he saw him
get into his car and start it up. I'm pretty certain Ryland
didn't go straight home himself, I believe he picked Debbie
up and they went off somewhere. He probably didn't get
home till around seven or eight. I'm sure his wife had a
shrewd idea of what he was up to, but the last thing she wants
is for it to come out into the open, to be forced into taking
some kind of attitude to it again.'

'You believe Fletcher was responsible for Helen's pregnancy?'

'Undoubtedly. When she worked for him he saw she was a
smart girl—and a good-looking one. He made her a prop-
osition and she jumped at it. He set her up in the flat, paid her
well. She was working on his books, helping him to run some
kind of fiddle, half a dozen different kinds of fiddle, most
likely. Fletcher operates in a very fertile field for rackets of
one kind or another: housing, development, planning, council contracts, improvement grants, VAT frauds, National
Insurance dodges, Income Tax. The scope's limitless.'

They reached the police station. Lambert drove on to the
forecourt and switched off the engine. 'Then Helen got
pregnant,' Kelsey said. 'Just about the time Woodroff was
persuading Fletcher to take a serious interest in politics.
Fletcher realizes Helen could prove a liability in the future.
He pays for the abortion and tells her the time has come to
end their arrangement. But she isn't to be disposed of so
easily. She's well aware what harm she could inflict on his
public and private life if she chose to open her mouth, she
isn't going to sell her silence cheaply. She tells him she wants
a handsome settlement, a flat or cottage perhaps, a new
car.

'He knows she won't be able to resist coming back for
more, there will never be an end to her demands. He's not the
sort of man to embark on a political career with that sort of
time-bomb ticking away underneath him. So he says: Sure,
no problem, we'll arrange it all amicably. Leave it to me, I'll

find you a nice little place. And there'll be a new car waiting
for you the day you move in.'

'I suppose it's possible,' Lambert said.

'It's a damn sight more than possible. It's what
happened—near enough. I'll take my oath on that.' He
frowned. 'That place Fletcher's people owned, in Devon or
Cornwall—'

'Ebrington Hall,' Lambert supplied.

'Find out where it is. Get down there tomorrow. Have a
ferret round.'

Several phone calls later Lambert was in possession of the
necessary information: there was a village named Ebrington
ten miles inland from the north coast of Devon. There had
at one time been an Ebrington Hall, a dwelling of some
antiquity, parts of it dating back to Tudor times. The hall
was no longer standing; it had been demolished some years
ago.

It was a beautiful bright blowy afternoon as Lambert struck
inland from the coast road. The spring was considerably
more advanced down here. Hawthorn stood in full snowy
splendour along the lanes, the banks were starred with
primroses and violets, blue speedwell, purple vetch.

He found the village without difficulty. A small pub stood
on the edge of the green. It was closed after lunch but as he
walked across to it a young woman came out of a side door
and shook a duster. He went over and told her he was trying
to trace any surviving members of the family who had lived
in Ebrington Hall.

'I'm sorry,' she said. 'I wouldn't know anything about
that, we haven't been here very long.' She thought for a
moment. 'You could go and see Mrs Gwynne. I know she
used to work at the Hall, she was there a long time. She won't
mind you calling, I'm sure. She's a widow, she lives on her
own, about a mile from here.' She gave him directions. 'I
dare say she'll be glad of a chat.'

Mrs Gwynne's cottage was an old farm dwelling, standing on its own at the end of a rutted lane. Lambert left the car near the entrance to the lane and walked down to the cottage; he could see smoke curling from a chimney. As he approached he heard a rhythmic beating sound coming from the rear of the dwelling. He walked round the side of the cottage and saw, a few yards away, a sturdy-looking woman in an overall, her hair tied up in a scarf, thumping energetically with a cane beater at a carpet draped over a washing line. Clouds of dust rose into the air and she was suddenly forced to abandon her beating because of a sharp fit of sneezing. Lambert moved into her field of vision and stood waiting till the fit had abated.

'My word! That's dusty work!' she exclaimed, laughing and dabbing at her nose. She didn't seem at all put out at seeing a total stranger, she gave him a glance of friendly inquiry from shrewd grey eyes.

Lambert apologized for disturbing her and explained his errand. 'They told me at the pub that you used to work at the Hall,' he added.

Mrs Gwynne smiled with reminiscent pleasure. 'I certainly did.' She glanced up at the sky, cast an eye over the carpet. 'That won't come to any harm for a few minutes. Come along inside, I'll make a cup of tea.' He followed her into the cottage, into a tiny hallway with a stag's head gazing out from above a door with a look of philosophical detachment. 'That came from Ebrington Hall,' Mrs Gwynne said. 'I had one or two things from there when the place was sold up. For old times' sake.' She took him into a little kitchen. 'Have you got some particular reason for wanting to know about the family?' she asked as she took cups and saucers from a corner cupboard.

'Legal business,' Lambert told her. That seemed to satisfy her, she gave a little nod.

'They told me at the pub that you worked for the Fletchers for several years,' he said.

She was filling a sugar bowl. She paused and glanced up at him. 'Fletchers?' she echoed. 'The family at the Hall wasn't called Fletcher. They were called Preston.' She saw his look of surprise. 'I know what it is,' she added with a half-smiling look, pleased at her own percipience. 'You've come across John Preston Fletcher. He told you his family lived up at the Hall.'

He moved his head in acquiescence.

She gave him a sharp glance. 'Is that what your legal business is about? Something to do with John Preston Fletcher?'

He said nothing but gave her an apologetic look.

'Don't tell me,' she said with amusement. 'Your lips are sealed.'

'The names make no difference,' he told her. 'I'd still like to know about the Prestons. And the Fletchers.'

'You've come to the right person,' she declared with energy. 'Nothing I like better than talking about old times. Don't get much of a chance these days, people think you're a bore if you start on about them.'

She made the tea and set out shortbread on a plate. 'It's homemade, freshly baked,' she assured him. 'None of your shop-bought stuff.' He took a piece; it was excellent, rich and buttery. 'I was cook at the Hall,' she said with pride. 'I started off as a kitchen maid but I was cook for a good ten years. I went there straight from school, that was a few years before the war.'

She sighed. 'The war made a lot of difference to the Prestons. They lost nearly all their money, most of it had come from places like Burma and Malaya.'

'Did the Prestons have any children?' Lambert asked.

She drank her tea. 'They only ever had the one child, a son. Andrew, his name was. He was a nice enough lad, good-looking too. A bit headstrong, but he'd have grown out of that—if he'd lived. He was killed in a hunting accident a few years after the war. He broke his neck, died all in a moment. He was only just nineteen.'

She sat in silence, cradling her cup in her hands. 'It was a terrible blow to his parents. Mrs Preston died a year or two later. She was never all that strong and it just about finished her off. It took all the heart out of her. She used to stay up in her room a lot, didn't want to go out anywhere. Then she got 'flu. It was a very hard winter that year, a lot of illness. She didn't make any kind of fight against it, she just let herself slip away. Mr Preston took it very hard, losing his son and then his wife. He closed up most of the rooms, cut right down on the staff, let the gardens go. He lived on for another eight or nine years, he more or less just faded away in the end. By that time it had got down to me and a daily woman, one gardener, and a lad for the odd jobs.'

She shook her head. 'I could shed a tear now, thinking about it. It was all so different when I first went there, there was plenty of life about the place then.' She sighed. 'Ah well, it does no good to keep looking back. Things alter and the world changes, and that's all there is to it.'

'And the Fletchers?' Lambert prompted.

She looked up at him with a return of vivacity. 'Oh yes, the Fletchers,' she said with a little grin. 'A different kettle of fish altogether. Ida Fletcher came to the Hall a year or two after me, as a housemaid. We were more or less the same age.'

She made a little face. 'I liked her well enough. We got on all right, but we were never what you would call bosom pals. I didn't approve of some of her ways. She was a very smart-looking girl, very handsome and full of life, tall, with a very good figure.' She sat back in her chair. 'About a month or two after young Andrew Preston broke his neck we could all see plain enough that Ida was in the family way. She never said a word about it to the rest of us. She left the Hall and went back to her parents, in the village. Her father had a smallholding, very decent sort of people they were.

'When the baby was born, a fine strong boy, she had him christened John—that was after her father and grandfather, all the Fletchers called the firstborn son John. John Preston Fletcher, that was what she had him christened.' She gave him a deeply significant look. 'I ask you—what were any of us supposed to make out of that?'

'What did you make out of it?' Lambert asked.

She made a dismissive gesture. 'It was as plain as the nose on your face what she wanted us to think: that young Andrew Preston was the baby's father.'

'Did you think he was?'

She shook her head with vigour. 'Not from anything I ever saw or had wind of. Nor any of the other servants at the Hall. Oh, I dare say Andrew had an eye for a pretty face as well as the next young man, and maybe she led him on a bit, she was certainly capable of that.' She pursed her lips. 'But she'd been sweet for I don't know how long on a man who worked at the big house in the next village, a chauffeur by the name of Endicott, a married man with a family. I know for a fact she used to meet him regularly on the sly, though she did her best to keep it dark. I reckon it was to put a stop to any gossip about the pair of them that she had the daft notion of calling the baby Preston. That's just the sort of thing that would strike her as clever, with Andrew being dead and buried, and in no position to deny anything.'

'I take it the Prestons knew what name the child was given?' Lambert said.

She gave a brisk nod. 'They certainly did. They'd have heard about it post haste from the Vicar if from nobody else. It was the talk of the village.' She looked earnestly up at him. 'I'm positive in my own mind it helped to kill Mrs Preston.'

'Did the Prestons tackle Ida about it?'

She shook her head. 'Not as far as anyone knew. After all, she didn't come out into the open and actually say Andrew was the father. If they had challenged her I suppose she could have said she'd named the child after the family as a mark of respect, or because she'd spent some happy years at the Hall, some tale like that. She'd have been quite capable of it, looking them straight in the face, she'd have thought that very amusing. I don't really see what they could have done about it. As far as I know, you can christen a child any name you please and you don't have to go round afterwards explaining why you chose it.'

'What happened to Ida after the baby was born?'

'She broke off with Endicott—or he broke off with her, I don't rightly know which way round it was. Anyway, she left the village, left the baby with her parents and went off and got herself a job. She had half-a-dozen different jobs in the next few years. Not in private houses—in shops, factories, hotels. She used to send money back for the child and every so often she'd come home to see him.'

She poured more tea. 'After a while she started coming back less and less. Her parents didn't mind, they'd been dreadfully upset over the whole business, they were just as pleased for her to stay away from the village. And they were very fond of the lad, they'd never had a son of their own. They never held it against him, like some folk would have done, the way he'd come into the world.'

'Who did the boy look like?' Lambert asked.

She gave him a knowing glance. 'There were a good many folk round here asking themselves that as the years went by.' She frowned a little. 'In the main I thought he took after his mother's family, he looked like his grandfather as much as anyone. I certainly never saw the slightest trace of the Prestons in him.'

She gave a sagacious nod. 'But I could see that chauffeur Endicott in him all right. Endicott was a fine-looking man, tall and well built. The boy had the same colouring, and he had a definite look of him round the nose and mouth.'

She tilted her head back. 'But where I really could see Endicott was in the boy's manner as he got older. Endicott always had a very frank, open way with him, he used to look at you very straight and direct, as if you were the only person in the world.' She smiled. 'He could charm the birds off the trees if he put his mind to it. And the boy had something of that same way with him. He was eighteen or nineteen when he finally left the village and by that time I could see it stronger than ever.' She finished her tea, set her cup down on its saucer with a little clatter. 'Oh no,' she said with finality, 'there was never any doubt in my mind who was the father of Master John Preston Fletcher.'

'Is Ida Fletcher still alive?' Lambert asked.

She pulled a face. 'For all I know, she is. She hasn't been back here for years. Her mother died when the boy was twelve or thirteen. Ida came back for her funeral, but she never offered to stay on and keep house for her father and the boy. I don't know that her father would have wanted it if she had offered. He had another daughter, married to a local farmworker. She was a few years older than Ida. They'd never got on well, she always thought Ida very selfish and flighty, and she was terribly shocked at all the business over the baby—particularly as she'd never managed to have any of her own, for all she was respectably married.

'Anyway, Ida took herself off after the funeral and left her father and the lad on their own. They got on well enough. Ida's sister used to call in and keep an eye on them. She'd do a bit of cooking and baking, see to their washing, all that kind of thing. Ida never came back again and after a time, from what her sister told me, the money stopped coming too.'

'Have you any idea what became of her?'

'There was a woman from round here, she went down to Southsea for a holiday one year. I don't know if you know Southsea, it's near Portsmouth. One day she went into Portsmouth and she saw Ida Fletcher getting into a car. A big posh car with a man driving it. She said he looked well-to-do, and he was making a big fuss of Ida. Ida was very well dressed, smart as paint.' She pursed her lips. 'I don't think anyone need worry their head about Miss Ida Fletcher. She'll always fall on her feet.'

'Did Mr Preston take any notice of the boy?'

'No, never. Of course the lad couldn't help but hear the gossip about his birth, he'd hear it from the other kids at school, if nowhere else. He certainly never set foot in the Hall by invitation of Mr Preston, but he did come sneaking round there once or twice while I was still working at the Hall. I caught him myself a few times and sent him about his business.' She shook her head slowly. 'It's hard to say what ideas a lad like that might get into his head.' She looked at Lambert with curiosity. 'You know him, do you?'

'I've come across him.' She waited for a moment but he didn't enlarge.

'He helped his grandfather on the smallholding all the time he was growing up,' she went on, 'and when he left school he worked on it full time. His grandfather believed in hard work and plenty of it, no fancy frills, but the lad never seemed to resent that, he took to the life naturally. He always seemed fond of his grandfather, they got on well. His grandfather certainly thought the sun shone out of that lad's eyes.'

She smiled. 'I remember once, when he was about fourteen, he was chopping swedes one day and he sliced the tip off one of his fingers.' She stuck out the middle finger of her left hand. 'He didn't make a fuss, he took it in his stride, but his grandfather was that upset, you'd have thought the lad was going to die. I told him: Just you be thankful it's nothing worse, not like that chap in the next village, lost his right arm in the threshing-machine.'

'Is the old man still alive?' Lambert asked.

'No, he isn't. He died when the boy was eighteen or so. Not that he was any great age, he wasn't much more then than I am now. He'd been getting a bit of arthritis, nothing very terrible, but it gave him gyp on and off, stopped him sleeping. He had some tablets from the doctor to ease the pain. That would be about the October. Then, when it came to the New Year's Eve, the boy brought home a bottle of whisky and the pair of them sat up drinking it—they were neither of them drinkers in the ordinary way. I suppose the lad fancied it would be a very grown-up thing to do, treat the old man to a bottle of whisky to see the New Year in.'

She stared back at the past. 'The married daughter looked in next morning to wish them both a happy New Year. The lad was still sleeping it off, right as rain, but the old man was dead in his bed.'

She sighed. 'They had an inquest of course, a post mortem and all that. They said it was Misadventure. The pills they used to give folk then, the painkillers, they weren't the same as they give you these days, it didn't take much of an overdose then to see you off. From what they said at the inquest, it seemed if you took too many, they stopped you breathing. And of course, drinking whisky, he never should have done that when he was taking the pills.

'It seems he'd taken quite a few more pills than his usual dose. They thought maybe he'd got confused from the whisky, forgot if he'd taken the pills. They were pretty sure it wasn't suicide. He didn't leave a note and he didn't seem to have any sort of reason for killing himself. The arthritis wasn't that bad and it didn't bother him after he had the tablets. He didn't have any money worries and he never seemed depressed or anything like that. He seemed pretty content with his life and he was happy with his grandson, no rows or disagreements.'

'Did his grandson give evidence at the inquest?'

'Oh yes. He was terribly upset, blamed himself, said he had no idea the pills shouldn't be taken with alcohol and so on. He made a very good impression, spoke up well, very straightforward, didn't try to wriggle out of anything. And everyone knew he'd been very fond of his grandfather.' She moved her head. 'Ida never came back, not even for the funeral, she never even wrote. I suppose it's possible she didn't know about any of it—no one knew where to write, to get hold of her. But it was in the papers, the county paper as well.'

'What happened to the smallholding?'

'The old man had made a will, he made it after his wife died. Everything was split right down the middle, half to his married daughter and half to his grandson. He never mentioned Ida in the will. The lad didn't want to stay on and try to run the smallholding himself, so they put the place up for sale right away. It fetched a very good price. It had been well looked after and the house was a solid little property, very well built. Even the old bits of furniture, stuff that had been in the family for generations, stuff none of us had ever valued, the dealers paid terrible fancy prices for it. I can tell you it made me look at some of my old bits and pieces when I heard what his stuff had fetched.

'And the old man had always been very thrifty. He'd saved quite a bit over the years, more than any of us would ever have thought. The moment the married daughter got her share she and her husband upped sticks and left the village. She'd never liked living in a tied cottage and he wasn't a skilled man, he was no more than a farm labourer. They went off to Exeter and opened a bed and breakfast place. They're doing well from what I've heard. They've never set foot in the village since.'

'And the grandson?'

'He was off like a shot as well. He went to Bristol, went into business there, set up on his own, young as he was.'

'I take it the Hall was closed up by then?' Lambert said.

'Oh yes. Old Mr Preston had been dead some years by that time. They closed the Hall after he died. I was working there right up to the end. The only relative he had left was an old lady up in Scotland, some cousin, older than him. She was bedridden, in a nursing home. She couldn't be bothered with any of it. She wasn't interested in the Hall, she hadn't set eyes on it for over forty years.'

'What happened to the place?'

'The old lady sent instructions that everything was to be sold, lock, stock and barrel. The land was easy enough to sell, a couple of local farmers bought that. And they sold off the

furniture and the rest of the stuff, but they couldn't find a
buyer for the Hall. It was too big, too out of the way, and it
had got into a pretty bad state, it would have cost a fortune to
put right. So it just stood empty. It went more and more
downhill and in the end it was pulled down.'

She drew a quavering sigh. 'I walk up there sometimes.
You can still make out the shape of the house on the ground,
where the different rooms used to be. And the pets' cemetery,
under the beech trees, the stones are still there, with all the
names on them.' She fell silent for a moment.

'I got married soon after Mr Preston died. I'd been
courting long enough, a cowman from one of the local farms.
We never had any children.' She smiled. 'I reckon we'd left it
a bit late.'

Lambert pushed back his chair and stood up. 'What was
your opinion of the grandson?' he asked.

'He was a hardworking lad, always well mannered, everyone liked him. I never heard a word or a whisper against
him.'

She hesitated. 'Perhaps I shouldn't say this, but you've
asked me a question and I'll answer it. It was that business
when his grandfather died, it always stuck in my mind. The
old man had never been used to drink, and it was the lad who
brought home that bottle of whisky. One day he was just a
country lad, working all hours on a smallholding, leading a
hard and simple life, at the beck and call of a grandfather
who could be expected to live another fifteen or twenty years.
Nine months later he was in Bristol with his own business,
riding around in a motor-car, living like a gentleman.' She
looked up at Lambert. 'It struck me at the time—and once or
twice since—that it all worked out very fortunate for John
Preston Fletcher.'

CHAPTER 13

The cottage pie that Lambert's landlady had left in the oven for him was more than a little dried up by the time he got back to Cannonbridge, but he made short work of it all the same before taking himself off to bed, where he fell at once into a deep and dreamless sleep.

He was at the station early next morning but the Chief was there ahead of him. He listened with keen attention to Lambert's account of his visit to Devon, jerking up his head with sharp interest when the sergeant described the circumstances surrounding the death of Fletcher's grandfather. But he made no comment.

When Lambert had finished Kelsey sat rubbing his chin for some moments, then he shook his head as if to clear it. 'I had a snoop round myself yesterday,' he told Lambert. 'I had a word with one or two folk about Woodroff.' A very discreet word, of course. And an even more discreet word about Fletcher. 'Fletcher started business leasing out office furniture and equipment.' His instinct appeared to be for diversification, he had branched out before long into hiring out machinery and general equipment. He seemed to have a natural talent for business, he had ridden the ups and downs of the stop-go years with inborn flair. 'He did well out of the tail end of the boom and he did even better out of the recession.' Then it was the buying up of bankrupt stock of all kinds, in particular machinery for resale abroad.

At various times he bought for a knock-down price some small business on the verge of folding, subjected it to rigorous pruning and modernization, brought it back into profitability. All these businesses were now running well, all meshing together to form a small but highly efficient empire. The plastics firm in Cannonbridge he had built from scratch, making shrewd use of grants from central Government as well as financial inducements offered by the local council. 'He has contracts with several councils in the area,' Kelsey said. 'A finger in a great many pies.'

As far as the Chief could make out, Fletcher's marriage seemed to be very soundly based. 'He's been married six years or so,' he told Lambert. Veronica Woodroff had been keeping house for her father when she met Fletcher. Her mother had belonged to a county family, had been active in various causes. When she died, Veronica—the Woodroffs' only child—had just left finishing school. She had taken on as many of her mother's commitments as she could cope with. 'She inherited a sizable fortune from her mother,' Kelsey said, 'and one day she'll come in for another, a good deal larger, from her father.' She had nothing to do with any aspect of Fletcher's businesses, she left all that to her husband; she concentrated on the social and political side of things, where she was a considerable help to Fletcher.

By all accounts Woodroff had a very high opinion of Fletcher. 'He looks on him as a son,' Kelsey said. 'Predicts a bright future for him in public life.' Woodroff's influential contacts must be an incalculable asset to a man with no secure background of his own. 'Apparently Fletcher has let it be understood in his circle that he's a by-blow of an old West Country family. Woodroff thinks no less of him for that. He admires Fletcher's drive, the way he's got on, battled against difficult beginnings.'

Kelsey got to his feet and began to pace about his office. 'It all points to crooked dealings of one kind or another,' he said. 'It's the only logical explanation for why he killed Helen Mowbray.'

'If he killed her,' Lambert ventured.

Kelsey flashed him a single glittering look. 'Oh, he killed her all right,' he said with total conviction. 'He killed them both. And his grandfather. I've not the slightest doubt he helped the old man on his way.' He had not an iota of proof, nothing that would stand up for thirty seconds in a court of law, but he was certain of it all the same. He knew it by all his years in the Force, by every nerve and instinct, by the smell and feel of it, by looks and pauses, things half-said or not said at all. And most particularly he knew it by the ripple along his spine when Fletcher held out the packet of mints to him over the office desk.

He struck his fists together. 'If we could just get a squint at his books.' The moment he had anything in the way of hard evidence he'd have men in combing through everything. 'There must be someone we can get at. Someone who knows or guesses something, someone who'll talk.'

There seemed little point in tackling Fletcher's secretary, Mrs Ogilvie. 'I very much doubt she's in on anything crooked,' Kelsey said. She had struck him as a very straightforward person; she had the look and manner of one speaking the truth, with nothing to hide. Discreet inquiries had tended to bear out that impression. She appeared to be happily married, two children doing well at school, her husband in a steady, well-paid job; they shared several interests. She seemed to lead a busy, settled, satisfactory life with no dark corners, no intolerable stresses.

'What about Ryland?' Lambert suggested.

Kelsey shook his head. 'I very much doubt Ryland's privy to all Fletcher's secrets.' He saw Fletcher as essentially a loner. 'He probably does all the necessary paperwork himself now. He'd have done it himself before Helen Mowbray came on the scene.' He'd have learned his lesson from that, not to trust anyone in that area again, not worth the risk. 'There's Mrs Stockman,' he said musingly. 'She might know or suspect something.'

'She was always employed in the general office,' Lambert reminded him. 'She'd hardly be likely to know anything.' If there's anything to know, he added to himself.

'She's an intelligent woman,' Kelsey argued. 'She may

have spotted something.' He's clutching at straws, Lambert thought.

Kelsey reached a decision. 'Right then—give Mrs Stockman a ring, see if she can spare us five minutes.' He sat down at his desk and picked up a sheaf of papers. He began to look through them.

Lambert got slowly to his feet. Kelsey glanced up at him. 'Get a move on,' he said sharply. 'You might catch her before she gets properly started for the day.' As Lambert reached the door Kelsey added, 'And don't be too fussy about fixing a time. We'll get over there whatever time she can see us— three o'clock in the morning if we have to.'

In the event it was two in the afternoon when they drove in through the farm gates. Mrs Stockman, busier than ever with the pageant, gave them coffee in the kitchen. 'You won't mind me carrying on with one or two little cooking jobs while we talk,' she said.

Kelsey waved a hand. 'Go right ahead.' She picked up a knife and began to peel and chop cooking apples with great speed. 'If you would cast your mind back to your days at Fletcher's,' Kelsey said. 'You were there some time?'

'Five years,' she told him.

'Did you ever come across anything that suggested to you, however slightly, that there might be something going on in the way of shady practices? Phoney accounts? Illegal dealings of any kind?'

'I never handled accounts,' Mrs Stockman said at once. 'I'm not much good with figures.'

'Did you ever see or hear anything at all,' Kelsey pressed her, 'that gave you the slightest reason to suppose that any aspect of Fletcher's business was not one hundred per cent above board?'

She paused in her task. 'There was just one very tiny incident.' She resumed her swift chopping. 'It was very likely nothing at all.'

'Tell us,' Kelsey urged her. 'We'll be the judges of that.'

She finished the apples and began to rub fat into flour. 'There was this woman, Mrs Lennox, she worked at the next desk to me. She wasn't there long, two or three months—this would be five or six years ago. She was quite a bit older than me, she'd be thirty-five or forty then. She was divorced, she had two children. She worked at Fletcher's part-time, she came in mornings. She worked on accounts, she'd been trained as a book-keeper before she was married. She was always in a terrible rush. She'd come flying in at the last moment, or five minutes late. And she was always off like a shot at lunch-time, trying to fit in a bit of shopping before she had to pick up the younger child from a minder. I didn't know her very well. She never had time for a chat and we didn't have much in common.' She began to roll out her pastry. 'On this particular day I'd just stood up to get something from a filing cabinet. I was going past her desk and I heard her say, "That's odd." I stopped and said, "What is?" It was the way she said it, more to herself than to me, slow and serious. She had two papers, one in each hand, she was comparing them.'

'Did she answer your question?'

'No. She noticed me standing there, she glanced up at me. I asked her again, "What's odd?" She stared at me and then she said, "Oh, I don't suppose it's anything. There's sure to be some perfectly simple explanation." I went off to the filing cabinet and she took the papers and went along to Mr Fletcher's office. She came back a few minutes later and got on with her work.'

'Did she refer to it again?'

'No. I wasn't all that interested. I don't suppose I'd have understood what she was talking about if she had tried to explain—she knew I was a dummy with figures.' She took a pie dish from a cupboard and greased it.

'Did you notice anything about the papers she was looking at? Anything at all?'

She closed her eyes in thought. 'Just that one of the two

papers was different from the rest.'

'In what way different?'

'A different colour, printed in different colour ink, set out differently. I got the impression that a stray had got in among the lot she was dealing with.'

'And that's the only thing that ever struck you as odd?'

She hesitated. 'No, not quite, there was something else. Mrs Lennox finished at Fletcher's at the end of that week, a couple of days after the incident with the papers. I thought it was very sudden.'

'Was she sacked?'

'Not exactly. She'd been taken on on a trial basis, to see if it would work out satisfactorily, with her being part-time and having the two children—none of the other clerks in the office was in the same kind of circumstances and Jack Ryland was a bit dubious about taking her on in the first place, he'd wondered if she'd be able to cope. But she was so keen to get the job and she was well qualified, she'd had very good experience before she was married, so he'd decided to give her a try. When she was paid at the end of that week Ryland told her he was sorry, but he didn't feel it was working out. She was a poor time-keeper and she always seemed to have a lot on her mind, she'd made mistakes through lack of concentration.'

'What was your opinion of her work?'

'I wasn't qualified to have an opinion of it. But she certainly wasn't a good time-keeper and she did always give the impression that half her mind was somewhere else.'

'She wasn't given any notice?'

'No, but she was paid a week's wages in lieu. She seemed satisfied with that. She didn't seem to think it was unfair to dismiss her, she seemed to think what Ryland said was quite justified.'

'But you still felt there was something unusual in the way she was asked to leave?'

'I did just wonder—' She paused.

'What did you wonder?'

'If she'd seen something she wasn't supposed to see.'

'Did she make any remark to you along those lines?'

She shook her head. 'But as I said, we didn't chat much. All she said was: I shan't be sorry to leave, it's been a hectic couple of months. The only thing I'll miss is the money.'

'Do you know where she is now?'

'I'm afraid not. I saw her once or twice in Cannonbridge after she left Fletcher's, and about a year later I saw her photo in the local paper, standing outside the register office. She'd got married again. Her husband looked an ordinary, decent type, middle-aged. Some address over in Martleigh, from what I remember.' She crossed to the stove and stirred a couple of pans.

'You don't by any chance remember his address?'

'No, I'm sorry.'

'Or his name?'

'I'm afraid not.'

'Do you know where she was living in Cannonbridge while she was working at Fletcher's?'

'Yes, she was living in Manor Road. I don't know the number.' She glanced up at the clock.

Kelsey pushed back his chair. 'You've been very helpful,' he told her. 'It's much appreciated.'

She turned from the stove. 'I suppose you know Fletcher has a weekend cottage?'

Kelsey stood motionless. 'No, we didn't know.' As he spoke the words he had a sudden recollection, that first time they'd spoken to Fletcher in his office, he'd said something then about being down at the cottage over Easter.

Mrs Stockman picked up her pie dish from the table and put it in the oven. 'He bought the cottage while I was working at Fletcher's,' she said. 'That would be about four years ago, a couple of years after Fletcher got married. I've never seen the cottage, of course, but they talked about it in the office when he was buying it. I stopped one day and had a

look at the photos in the estate agent's window. Providence
Cottage, it's called. It's a small place, pretty old. There's
some land with it, some woodland, and a trout stream.'

'Whereabouts is it?'

She gave him details of the location, a mile or so outside a
small village some eight miles to the south-west of Cannonbridge.

'We'll get over there now and take a look round,' Kelsey
said to Lambert as they got into the car. He sat studying the
map as Lambert drove out through the gates. 'Stoneleigh's
only a couple of miles from Fletcher's cottage,' he said after a
minute or two. He looked up from the map. 'That's where he
killed them both,' he said with absolute certainty. 'In the
cottage grounds.'

A lane turned off the road on the left. A little way along it
another, narrower, lane ran off to the right; it was signposted
to Providence Cottage.

They passed a field of cattle grazing in the sunshine, an
orchard of damson trees in blossom, a hazel coppice breaking
into leaf. There was no sign of any other dwelling.

A five-barred gate gave entry to the cottage grounds. They
left the car drawn tight up against the gate and walked along
a winding path that took them through a rough field, a
paddock, a shrubbery, and round to the front of the cottage,
solidly built of stone. The doors and windows were closed,
there was no sign of life. They could hear a murmur of
running water away on the right where the land sloped
down, no doubt to the bank of the trout stream. Some
distance behind the cottage was a stretch of greening woodland. April sun gilded the sky; the voices of blackbird and
thrush sounded sweetly from the budding trees.

Kelsey remained for some little time glancing about in
silence, then, still in silence, he turned and walked slowly
back to the car.

★

Shortly before half past five Sergeant Lambert went along to Manor Road. He found a newsagent's a couple of streets away and inquired if they knew of a Mrs Lennox.

Yes, they had known her well, she had bought her papers from them for years. 'But she's left here now,' the newsagent's wife told him. 'She got married again a few years ago, she went over to Martleigh to live.' No, she didn't know her address in Martleigh, nor the name of her new husband, but she could tell him whereabouts in Manor Road Mrs Lennox had lived. 'Number 46. It's a semi, there's a big sycamore in the front garden.'

As Lambert walked up the path of No. 46 he could hear from an upstairs room the sound of an infant crying, the steady, relentless crying of a baby that has long forgotten why it is crying and is now close to exhaustion. He pressed the bell and after some delay the door was jerked open by a flushed, harassed-looking young woman who appeared on the verge of tears herself.

'Yes?' She threw him a distracted, unwelcoming glance. He revealed his identity and explained his business as swiftly as possible. All the while the baby kept up a hopeless, heartbroken bawling, like a lost soul in Hades.

She pulled the door back. 'You'd better come in.' She flung him a despairing glance. 'You wouldn't know anything about babies?'

'I'm afraid not,' he told her. 'I'm not married.'

She closed the door behind him. 'I'd better fetch him down or we won't be able to hear ourselves speak. I've been trying to get him to go off for the past half-hour. My sister's coming over at seven o'clock to babysit. We're supposed to be going out this evening, a dinner-dance at my husband's firm.' She left him standing in the hall while she ran upstairs and into a bedroom. A moment later the howling died abruptly away.

She came out of the bedroom holding the baby up against her shoulder. She came down the stairs, talking to the child as she came. He emitted a series of mournful hiccups but otherwise appeared more resigned to life.

'You'd better come through here,' she told Lambert. He followed her into an untidy kitchen. 'Sit down,' she said. 'I'll have to deal with his lordship first.' She took a flannel from the draining-board and wiped the baby's tear-stained face. He seemed very small and frail for a creature capable of so much persistent uproar; Lambert judged him to be no more than a couple of months old.

The baby fell suddenly into an exhausted sleep, his head lolling against his mother's arm. 'Thank God for that,' she said with fervour. She patted his face dry with a towel and sat down at the table. 'I'm sorry about all that. Now, what was it you wanted to know? I'm afraid I've forgotten.'

'Mrs Lennox,' he said. 'She used to live here a few years back.'

'Oh yes, I remember her. We bought the house off her.' No, she couldn't remember her new name or her address in Martleigh. 'But she did leave me her address,' she recalled. 'In case any letters came for her.' She darted a look about the kitchen. 'She did have some odds and ends come for her. I sent stuff on for a year or more after she left.' She frowned. 'But that's going back a bit now. I haven't seen the card for ages. It was a business card she gave me, one of her husband's cards, he's in some business or other.'

She closed her eyes and tilted back her head. 'A shop, yes, that was it, a shoe shop, I'm pretty sure that's what it was.' She got to her feet. Still cradling the baby, she began to walk about the room, scanning every horizontal surface. 'It's here somewhere, I'm sure it is, I know I didn't throw it away.' With her free hand she opened a cupboard and made a half-hearted attempt to look through it. After a minute or two she abandoned the attempt and turned to face Lambert.

'Look,' she said with decision. 'I can't give my mind to it now. I've got half a dozen things I should be doing.'

Lambert stood up. 'We'd be very glad of the address,' he told her.

She gave an impatient nod. 'I will definitely look for it. As soon as I find it I'll phone the station or I'll drop it in if I'm passing.' She glanced at the clock; he saw her attention was already slipping away to more urgent matters.

He looked at the clutter on the shelves, on top of the fridge, the washing-machine, the dresser. 'It could be important,' he said without hope.

She glanced at him as if suddenly recalling his existence. 'I won't forget, that's a promise.' She urged him out of the kitchen, towards the front door. 'The first moment I've got, I'll find it. Don't you worry.'

Lambert returned to the station where the Chief greeted the results of his foray with a marked lack of warmth. 'You can get back there first thing tomorrow,' he ordered. 'She'll never give it another thought if you don't keep after her.'

When the alarm clock shrilled beside the Chief's bed next morning he came awake at once. Often when a case had reached a point where he found himself up against one brick wall after another—and particularly in a case where addition- ally he was chancing his arm—he woke to feel a crushing weight on his chest, as of a dog planted squarely on his breastbone. In the days when he was married he would lie tensely beside his sleeping wife, rigid with fear of an imminent heart attack.

But that was years ago. Now, long since divorced and on his own again, he had grown accustomed to the sensation. It no longer scared the wits out of him, he acknowledged its re-appearance as he might a familiar acquaintance, if not precisely an old friend.

Sometimes—as on this particular morning—he woke to a more advanced stage of the disorder: the dog was still firmly planted on his chest but in addition a great and unremitting pressure was being applied to his ribs, which felt as if at any moment they might crack under the assault. But even this highly unpleasant variant no longer troubled him. After the first few horrid moments he was able to close his mind to it, having learned by now that all he had to do was throw back the covers and leap out of bed. In less than a minute dog and rib-crackers would have vanished.

He linked his hands behind his head and stared up at the shadowy ceiling. So far he had not an atom of proof that Fletcher had had any kind of contact with Helen Mowbray after she left the firm. He'd cherished great hopes of the antique gold-and-turquoise bracelet given to Helen, according to Mrs Cope, by the man responsible for her pregnancy—given to her in the summer, two or three months after she'd left Fletcher's. He was positive it was Fletcher who had given her the bracelet; if they could only establish that then they'd begin to get some solid ground under their feet.

Fletcher must have bought the bracelet somewhere. They'd had no results from inquiries at jewellers, antique shops, pawnbrokers in Cannonbridge; the more widely circulated police lists had produced nothing. More detailed inquiries were now moving further afield, to neighbouring towns.

He flung back the bedclothes and sprang out of bed. Five minutes later he was making toast and drinking tea in the kitchen of his flat. The weather had turned a good deal colder in the night, the wind had backed towards the north. It was a bright, invigorating morning; he felt brisk and alert, ready for another day.

This cheerful, braced feeling lasted until two minutes after he arrived at the police station. A message awaited him at the desk: Would he go along immediately to the Superintendent's office.

Oh-ho, Kelsey thought, sinking his teeth into his lip, Woodroff has spoken. He went smartly off along the corridor, keeping his mind blank and relaxed, ready to deal with whatever arrows the Super—a gentleman with whom he had had brushes before—might be disposed to fire at him. The Super was some years older than Kelsey, of a deeply conservative temperament, sprung from a deeply conservative background, reinforced by a deeply conservative education. He liked every step to be taken, every avenue to be explored—but he also, most emphatically, liked every rule to be kept.

When Kelsey reached his office the Super didn't invite him to sit down, nor did he remain seated himself. He got to his feet and strode across to the window. He stood with his back to it, his hands clasped behind him, frowning savagely at the Chief. There was silence for several seconds. Down in the street someone whistled a tune of the moment, clear and sweet.

The Super suddenly burst forth. A complaint had been made, a complaint such as the Super didn't care to hear of in connection with any of his men, most particularly not in connection with one of his senior officers. A strongly worded complaint of harassment, unreasonable invasion of domestic privacy. 'It's by no means the first time you've overstepped the mark,' the Super told him. 'I would most strongly advise you in your own interests to see that it is the last.'

The Chief made no response, knowing from harsh experience that no response was required or would be welcomed. He merely held himself in as neutral a stance as possible, staring straight ahead with as blank a gaze as he could muster.

These tactics worked to some extent. After a few minutes peppered with references to the Chief Constable, Woodroff and Fletcher, observations about zeal and enthusiasm being all very well in their way but not at the expense of discretion and common sense, together with a number of other sentiments along the same lines, some of the steam began to go out of the Super's utterances. He paused and drew a deep breath, his eyes looked marginally less baleful. 'I realize this is a difficult case,' he said in a slightly softened tone. 'It's very tempting to go charging into every possible opening.' He took a step forward into the room, adding in a more human voice, 'But it's no good going off at half cock. There's no sense in making enemies of local people, particularly not of prominent and influential local people.' He gave a long, loud sigh. 'There's no percentage in that at all.'

Sergeant Lambert didn't need to go back to Manor Road after all. When he walked into the station he also found a message waiting for him at the desk: a card had been handed in for him by a lady in the early hours of the morning. A very merry lady, apparently. She had just returned home after some festivity and had been struck, as by a bolt of lightning—so she had told the desk sergeant—by the recollection of where she had put the card Sergeant Lambert had been so anxious about. She had persuaded her husband to get the car out again and drive her to the station, where she had been very voluble, if not always very coherent, in her explanations.

Lambert looked at the card, a shiny, once-white oblong stained with old coffee splashes. It proclaimed in a curly script: A. L. Gillespie, 72 High Street, Martleigh. Ladies', Gents' and Children's Footwear. Difficult Fittings a Speciality.

He turned the card over. On the back was written in an unsteady, flamboyant hand: 'I did remember!' and underneath: 'Baby sends his apolgys.' This last word had been crossed out and replaced by a correction, alopogies, which had in turn been crossed out and replaced by the final decisive selection: AGOLOPIES, in large, triumphant capitals.

CHAPTER 14

The Chief came into Lambert's office as he was attempting for the fourth time to dial the number of Gillespie's shoe shop. For the fourth time the phone gave the engaged signal.

Lambert replaced the receiver. 'They could have left the phone off the hook,' he said. 'I'll give it another try.'

'Don't bother,' Kelsey told him. 'We'll get over there ourselves.' There were a dozen matters he should be attending to but he felt far too restless to remain in the station overseeing the routine drudgery of investigation; he must do something, anything, that appeared to offer even the faintest hope of leading to something positive.

During the journey he sat tense and silent. As they halted for traffic lights on the way out of Cannonbridge Lambert saw him turn his head to look at a poster advertising a meeting for seven-thirty that evening at the Memorial Hall. Fletcher's frank, square-jawed face smiled confidently out at them: high wide forehead, candid eyes, resolute, steadfast look. The Chief made no comment, he turned his head again and stared out at the traffic with an abstracted gaze.

Pallid sunlight glittered Martleigh High Street. Gillespie's shoe shop occupied a good position, close to a bus stop and not far from a municipal car park. The premises had clearly undergone considerable alteration in recent times and now sported a Continental look with gaily striped awnings, dwarf conifers in tubs on either side of the entrance, a general impression of pine, bamboo and canework in the interior décor. Subdued strains of popular music with a distinctly French flavour floated out into the street.

The shop was doing a lively trade but Gillespie, an affable, middle-aged man, was able to spare them a few minutes. Kelsey mentioned the case on which they were working and asked if he might speak to Mrs Gillespie. He understood she had at one time worked for a firm which had employed one of the dead girls; it was possible she might be able to give them useful information.

Gillespie listened with surprise and interest. They had read about the case in the papers, a dreadful, shocking business. His wife had been particularly interested, having lived in Cannonbridge for a number of years, but she had certainly had no idea that she might herself have been linked with any aspect of the case.

'I'm sure she'd be only too pleased to help you in any way she could,' he assured them. 'But I'm afraid she isn't here at the moment. She's in Europe, on a buying trip, she goes over there three or four times a year.' He waved a hand. 'She's revolutionized this business since we got married. It was all football boots and old ladies' runners before she took charge.'

Kelsey closed his eyes for a moment in acute disappointment. 'When will she be back?' he asked.

'On Saturday evening.'

'Will you be in touch with her before then?'

Gillespie shook his head. 'I don't expect to be. I don't even know for certain where she'll be at any given moment.' Yes, he would ask her to ring them as soon as she got back.

Throughout the return journey Kelsey again sat in brooding silence. When they reached the station he got slowly out of the car and went heavily up the steps towards the mountain of time- and energy-consuming detail that had lain inexorably in wait for him during his absence.

At a quarter to five, when Sergeant Lambert was beginning to think about calling it a day and getting off back to his digs, the door of his office burst open and the Chief came striding in with an air of suddenly renewed energy. He had despatched enough of the tedious chores to be able to leave the rest with a fairly free conscience until tomorrow. Or the day after.

Lambert glanced up at him without hope, knowing from the green glitter in the Chief's eyes and the pouncing little smile on his craggy features that wherever he, Sergeant Lambert, was about to go off to in the next couple of hours, it certainly wasn't going to be back to his digs.

'It stands to reason,' the Chief said, as if resuming a dialogue interrupted a moment before, 'that Mrs Fletcher must be lying about her husband's movements that Wednesday evening. We'll get over there now and tackle her about it.'

Lambert tried to say something about the lack of any real evidence, better perhaps to wait till they'd had a chance to talk to Mrs Gillespie. 'She might give us something a little firmer to work on,' he said. Or enable us to dismiss the whole bag of tricks as moonshine, he added to himself. 'Woodroff isn't going to be best pleased when he hears we've been over to Pearmain House again, as good as calling his daughter and son-in-law a pair of liars.' Even as he spoke he knew he was wasting his breath. The Chief was clearly in overdrive, he would plunge recklessly on, irresistibly impelled to the edge of the cliff—and possibly beyond.

The Chief gave him a blind, restless stare. 'To hell with Woodroff,' he said. 'We'll get over to Pearmain House now. We'll catch Mrs Fletcher before her husband gets home.'

Today there were no cars standing in the driveway when they reached Pearmain House. Mrs Fletcher answered their ring at the front door with an air of controlled haste as of someone disturbed while hard at work. She looked a trifle surprised to see them but stepped aside at once for them to enter. 'If you wouldn't mind coming along to the study,' she said as she preceded them along the passage. She gestured them into the room. 'You find me up to the eyes,' she added with a smile. She nodded at a desk with orderly piles of papers ranged beside a typewriter. A wooden tea-trolley nearby held bundles of newsletters, stacks of envelopes.

'You do a good deal to help your husband,' Kelsey remarked.

'One does what one can,' she replied briskly. 'One tries to pull one's weight. The election's only three weeks away.' She waved a hand, inviting them to sit down. 'I enjoy it all, it's no hardship.'

'This election means a lot to your husband,' Kelsey observed as he took a seat opposite her.

'It certainly does. It's only a local council, and not an important local council at that, but it's the first step for Preston, and that makes it very important to us.' She gave the Chief a rueful little smile. 'I'm afraid you've had a wasted journey. Preston isn't here. He won't be back till late this evening, not till about eleven. He's doing the rounds of his other businesses, then he's going straight along to the Memorial Hall.'

'Will you be going to the meeting?' Kelsey asked casually.

She shook her head. 'Nothing I'd like better, but at this stage it would be sheer self-indulgence, I simply can't afford the time. I'm going out canvassing, that's where I feel I can be of most use just now.'

'Will you be in touch with your husband in the course of the evening?' Kelsey's tone was even more casual.

Again she shook her head. Lambert saw the Chief sit back in his chair as if relaxing by ever so little.

'Perhaps as we are here,' Kelsey said, 'you might be able to help us with a couple of minor points that need clarifying.'

'By all means,' she said at once. 'If I can be of any assistance.'

'We're checking everyone's statements, right from the start, every last word of them. It's a tedious business but it's got to be done. Now—your husband's movements that Wednesday evening, March 2nd; if I could ask you to cast your mind back once again. I'm sure I don't have to explain how important it is to get every detail right in these matters. You're a woman with a civic conscience, you understand these things more than most. We're dealing with something of the utmost importance to the whole community, the brutal murders of two young women. With the best will in the world, when it comes to making statements, people do make mistakes, they do forget, and one tiny error can throw the whole picture out.'

She gave an impatient nod. 'Yes, I understand all that, I don't mind in the least.' She repeated without hesitation the substance of what she and Fletcher had already told the Chief.

'Would you consider the possibility,' the Chief suggested with a relaxed, detached air, 'that you might both be confusing that Wednesday evening with, say, the Tuesday or Thursday evening of the same week—or even perhaps with the Wednesday evening of the previous week or the following week? The memory can play that kind of trick. You'd be surprised how often we come across that particular sort of confusion when we take statements.'

'There's no possibility of confusion,' she told him with assurance. 'I'm quite certain about it. There are the diaries, you see. We're neither of us simply relying on memory.'

'I grant you that,' the Chief said with a judicial air. 'But would you perhaps consider whether your husband might have come home that Wednesday evening a little later than you've told us?'

'No, he didn't come home any later than I've told you,' she answered crisply. Lambert saw her eyes grow steely bright. 'We had arranged the night before that we'd make a start on the speech on the Wednesday evening, as soon as we'd eaten. I would certainly have remembered if he'd come home later than usual that evening. He did not. We ate and then we got straight down to work.'

'Did he perhaps go out again in the course of the evening?' Kelsey asked with unflagging persistence. 'It's possible it slipped your mind.'

'He very definitely did not go out again that evening.' She looked unwaveringly back at the Chief. 'It certainly wouldn't have slipped both our minds.' Kelsey's heart began to thump. Not a shadow of doubt about it, he thought; she's lying. She shows no anger at the line of questioning, she's poised and guarded, like a fencer.

He threw caution to the winds. 'Would you be prepared to

stand up in court and swear to all that?' Lambert closed his
eyes in dismay.

'Yes, of course,' she said, her tone edged with surprise.
'Though I can't see any conceivable reason why I should be
called on to do so.' She smiled slightly, her gaze still level and
unshaken. If she wasn't lying she'd pursue that, Kelsey
thought; she'd be indignant, outraged, she wouldn't just let it
lie there.

'If that's all then,' she said on a conclusive note, 'I really
must ask you to excuse me.' She glanced at the carriage clock
on the mantelshelf. 'I have to pick up another canvasser.' She
stood up. 'Mustn't be late, sets a bad example.' She gave him
a relaxed, friendly smile, displaying her regulated, pearly
teeth.

'She'll sing a different tune once we pull Fletcher in,'
Kelsey said sourly to Lambert as they got into the car.
'Woodroff will see to that, for all he thinks his son-in-law
such a fine young fellow now. He'll drop him pretty swiftly
when he discovers the truth. He and his precious daughter
won't be able to scramble clear of contamination fast
enough. Families like the Woodroffs didn't get where they
are by making common cause with murderers.'

Lambert started the engine. 'Right, then,' Kelsey said
with undiminished energy. 'Rylands' next stop. Ryland
couldn't have seen Fletcher actually drive off home that
Wednesday evening, he's got to be made to change his story.'
He sat back. 'He should be home by the time we get there.
We've never spoken to him and his wife together before. You
never know,' he added with unquenched optimism. 'It could
make all the difference.'

Over in the old part of Wychford, Detective-Constable Jago
was making his way back to the car park at the end of a day
he could only regard as one hundred per cent unsuccessful;
not a jeweller, shopkeeper or pawnbroker in the town had
recognized the gold-and-turquoise bracelet.

He blew out a long breath of frustration, glancing about as he went. On the other side of the road he noticed an alley in the middle of a terrace of shops. From force of habit he crossed over and stood looking down the alley. Half way along it he could see a watchmaker's sign above the window of a small, old-fashioned shop; the clock beneath the sign showed five twenty-five. He set off down the alley.

In the shop window were a number of antique watches and clocks, and, in the right-hand rear corner, a small glass case holding a dozen or so pieces of old jewellery. He pushed open the door and went inside.

The ping of the bell brought the shopkeeper out from the back premises; an elderly man with a shrewd, sharp face. He knew Jago for what he was before the constable began his spiel and produced the bracelet. He looked down at it with keen interest.

'Yes, I recognize it,' he said at once. 'And I remember the man I sold it to,' he added with a laugh. 'I won't forget him in a hurry. He beat me down forty pounds over that bracelet.' He looked up at Jago, his eyes amused. 'I never haggle in the ordinary way. I fix a price and that's that, they can pay it or not, as they choose.' He jerked his head. 'I consider myself a pretty sharp operator but he got the better of me over that and I don't mind admitting it.' He seemed illogically cheerful at the recollection.

He took the bracelet in its plastic wrapping, turned it over, scrutinized it. 'Yes, there it is.' He held it out under Jago's nose. 'I don't know if you can see that little repair on the back.' Jago could see nothing in the way of a repair. 'Ninety-nine people out of a hundred wouldn't see it either,' the shopkeeper assured him. 'I did that repair myself, made a pretty good job of it too. But he spotted it at once.'

'Can you tell me the date you sold the bracelet?' Jago asked.

'I'll get the book.' He disappeared into the rear quarters and returned a few moments later with a ledger which he set down on the counter. He turned the pages. 'Yes, here we are. June, two years ago.' He showed Jago the entry. 'You can see what I wrote there, about the price he paid me.'

'There's no name,' Jago said in sharp disappointment.

'No. He paid in cash, he didn't need to leave his name. I don't do any serious dealing in jewellery, I come by a few pieces now and then through the watches and clocks. The way I came by the bracelet—I bought a collection of time-pieces when an old lady died locally. Her son asked me to take a look at them and give him a price for the lot. While I was there he asked me if I'd look at some old jewellery his mother had. There was a boxful of the stuff, most of it sentimental rubbish, three or four good pieces in among it. That bracelet was one of them.'

'The man who bought the bracelet,' Jago said. 'Has he been in here since?'

The shopkeeper shook his head. 'Never seen him before or since.' He glanced up at Jago. 'But I'd know him again all right. You can bank on that.'

CHAPTER 15

Ryland was sitting at the kitchen table over his tea when the two policemen walked up the front path.

'You'll be off out helping with the canvassing, I expect?' Kelsey said jovially to him as he followed Mrs Ryland into the kitchen. A radio on the dresser disgorged gobbets of information and opinions on current affairs; from upstairs came the sound of a child squealing with laughter, a girl's voice calling out to him.

Ryland glanced up at the two men without enthusiasm. 'I'm not bothered about politics.' He stood up and switched off the radio, he returned to his seat at the table. 'Can't work up much of an interest, never have been able to.'

Mrs Ryland didn't ask them to sit down, didn't offer them tea. She began clearing the table round her husband. She didn't look at Ryland, didn't speak, but kept her eyes fixed on what she was doing, working with more noise and energy than the task appeared to warrant.

'And Mrs Ryland?' Kelsey said to her with relentless affability. 'Do you lend a hand with election chores?'

She made no reply, didn't glance at him, but continued with her bustle. 'She's the same as me,' Ryland said. 'She takes no interest in politics. Mr Fletcher doesn't mind, he's not short of willing helpers.' His manner became a fraction more relaxed. 'I take what I can off his shoulders at work. I look on that as playing my part.'

'Neither of you going to the meeting at the Memorial Hall, then?'

Ryland shook his head. He glanced up at the clock and uttered an exclamation. 'I'll have to get a move on. I'm running my daughter over to catch the motorway express.' He mentioned a pick-up point some miles away. 'She's off to stay with my sister and her family for a couple of days, before school starts again next week.' He set about the last of his meal with despatch. He didn't ask them why they had called. Mrs Ryland ran hot water into the sink, added a squirt of detergent and began to attack the crockery with a washing-up brush.

'We'd better get down to business, then,' Kelsey said amiably. 'If I could take you back again to that Wednesday evening.' Ryland's face assumed an expression of weary irritation. 'I'm hoping by now you may have remembered some detail, could be something that strikes you as very trivial but it might be just the piece we need.'

Ryland's expression grew stubborn. 'Fletcher and I left the office together that evening. We stood chatting for a minute or two, then we got into our cars and drove off.'

'Where did you drive off to?'

'Straight home. I've already told you all this.'

'You're sure you didn't turn right instead of left when you came out through the gates?'

'I most certainly did not. Why should I want to do that?' At the sink Mrs Ryland stood arrested. Upstairs the child sang a loud, garbled version of Three Blind Mice.

'You didn't fancy a little run up the road? Up into the hills, perhaps?'

Ryland's jaw set. 'No, I did not. I drove straight home.' Mrs Ryland's shoulders relaxed, she resumed her attack on the dishes.

'Who drove off first? You or Fletcher?'

There was a brief pause, then Ryland said, 'Fletcher did.'

'You actually saw Fletcher drive out through the gates and head for home?'

Another pause. 'Yes, I did,' Ryland said at length.

'You're sure of that?'

'Yes, I'm sure.' He spoke with assurance now. 'We take the same road home, he was in front of me all the way. I saw him continuing up the road when I turned in here.'

'You'd swear to that in court?'

'Yes, of course I would.' All hesitation had vanished. But I'm positive he's lying, Kelsey thought, I'd stake my last shilling on it. He's got to be lying, there's no other explanation. He could see by the set of Ryland's jaw that the more he pressed him on the point, the harder he would dig in his heels.

'Do you know of any connection between Helen Mowbray and Fletcher after she left the firm?' he asked. 'Do you know if she was employed to do any form of accounts or book-keeping after she left?'

Ryland sat very still. As if he's remembering something. Sergeant Lambert thought; as if two and two suddenly make four to him.

'Well?' Kelsey said.

Ryland shook his head. 'No, I'm not aware that she was ever employed like that after she left.'

Kelsey stood looking down at him for some moments, then he said abruptly, 'Did you know about her pregnancy?'

Ryland's face registered shock. At the sink there was sudden silence.

'No,' Ryland answered.

'You'd swear to that?'

'I certainly would. I knew nothing of any abortion.'

There was a palpable silence in the room. Upstairs the child sang and laughed.

'Who said anything about an abortion?' Kelsey asked.

Ryland shifted in his chair. 'You did. Just now.' Mrs Ryland stood frozen, her head lowered, her rubber-gloved hands gripping the sides of the sink.

'I made no mention of any abortion,' Kelsey said. 'I mentioned Helen Mowbray's pregnancy.'

'I'm sorry,' Ryland said in an uneven voice. 'I must have misunderstood you.'

'Did you in fact know she had an abortion?'

'I did not,' he said with force. 'Nor did I know about any pregnancy. I knew nothing about it till this moment.' Mrs Ryland began to wash up again, with a good deal less noise.

There was a sound of running footsteps and a girl of nine or ten came into the kitchen, very neatly dressed, with a bright, lively face. 'I'm ready, Dad!' she called as she came. She halted abruptly at the sight of the two men standing there. She threw them a single glance, not of curiosity or inquiry but of resentment and irritation, plainly fearing that their business, whatever it might be, could threaten her departure.

'Come on, Dad!' she urged him. 'We've got to go!' Her face grew flushed. She snatched up a coat that lay over the back of a chair and tugged it on.

'Yes, all right.' Ryland glanced from the two men to his wife who still stood with her back to them, busy with the dishes. 'If that's all, then,' he said to the Chief, clearly hoping the two of them would take themselves off.

Kelsey waved an amiable hand. 'Don't let us hinder you.

You get along and take your daughter to her bus.'

Ryland got slowly to his feet. The girl tugged at his sleeve, with signs of increasing agitation. He drew a long, resigned breath, stooped and picked up a suitcase standing by the wall. His wife turned from the sink and dried her hands. 'I won't be long,' he told her. She didn't look at the two policemen, she followed her husband and daughter to the front door; Lambert could hear the murmur of their voices. The car started up and moved off, the girl called back a shouted farewell. The front door closed again and Mrs Ryland came back into the kitchen.

'Right, then,' she said on a decisive note as she entered. 'You'll be off, I dare say.' She gave the Chief a challenging look.

'One or two details we'd like to check with you,' Kelsey told her. 'Then we'll get out of your way.' She set her lips in displeasure. 'It's the question of the time your husband came home that Wednesday evening.'

'Not again!' she burst out. 'I've already told you what time he came home, my husband's told you what time he came home, but it makes not a blind bit of difference. Why have you got it in for him?'

'No one's got it in for your husband,' Kelsey said dispassionately. 'No one is for one moment suggesting that he had anything to do with the deaths of those two girls. But we do have reason to suppose that he didn't come home that evening at the time you both say he did. I've no doubt you both have your reasons for saying what you did but it distorts our picture of what happened that evening.' She had begun to shake her head as soon as he started speaking, she continued to shake it. 'We've got to get at the truth,' Kelsey insisted. 'We believe the truth of the matter is that your husband—'

'I don't want to know about any of that!' she flung at him, her eyes flashing. 'I've been through all that, I don't want any more of it. You can stand there badgering me all night

but I won't change what I've told you. Now you can both
clear out and let me get on with my work.' She began with
furious movements to remove the remaining tea-things from
the table and carry them to the sink.

'Two young women have been brutally done to death,'
Kelsey said. 'One of them only a couple of years older than
your eldest daughter.'

'Those girls are dead,' she said with force. 'We've still got
our lives to lead. I stand by what my husband's told you and
I'll continue to stand by it.' She resumed her washing-up
with such vigour that splashes of sudsy water jetted up into
the air around her. Kelsey stood regarding her. She turned
her head and stared defiantly back at him. Her cheeks were
flushed, her eyes brilliant.

'If you change your mind,' Kelsey told her. 'If your
conscience starts to bother you, if you wake in the night and
remember your own daughters, you can always give us a
ring. Any time, night or day.'

When they were outside in the car again Lambert looked
at the Chief, expecting instructions. Kelsey said nothing but
sat with his head lowered and his eyes closed. Lambert
managed with difficulty to suppress his yawns.

'Better get back to the station,' Kelsey said at last. He
sounded immensely fatigued, flat and dejected.

Lambert turned the car in the direction of Cannonbridge.
The traffic had thinned after the early evening rush. Neither
of them spoke.

A little way along the road a boy came out of a chip shop
over on the left, and started to walk along the pavement
towards them. The Chief glanced out at him. 'Graham
Cooney,' Lambert told him. 'From the Parkfield estate.' As
they drew level Lambert raised a hand and grinned.
Graham's eyes met his but he didn't smile or return the
greeting, he continued stolidly on his way.

'What's got into him?' Kelsey asked.

'Search me,' Lambert said. 'He's been like that the last

couple of times I've come across him. He was friendly enough before.'

'Is that so?' Kelsey said sharply. 'Pull up.' The moment the car halted he jumped out and strode rapidly after the boy. 'Hello there,' he called out as he caught up with him. Graham halted but didn't turn round. He clutched the bag of fish and chips close to his chest; the savoury smell reached the Chief's nostrils.

'How's that young brother of yours these days?' the Chief asked amiably. 'Not doing any more running away?'

'He's all right,' Graham answered in a low, reluctant tone, staring fixedly ahead. The colour rose in his face.

'You're quite a way from home,' Kelsey remarked in a friendly manner. 'What are you doing round here?'

'I've been playing with some mates.'

'Live round here, do they?' Kelsey asked jovially. The boy said nothing. 'They have names, these mates of yours?' Still no reply. 'We can give you a lift home,' Kelsey offered. 'Won't be out of our way.'

Graham shook his head. 'No, thanks, I don't need a lift.'

'Where are you off to then? Parkfield's in the other direction.' Graham didn't answer. Kelsey stood looking at him but the lad remained silent and unyielding.

Kelsey turned and walked back to the car. He got in and directed Lambert to turn round and drive slowly back the way they had come. 'There he is!' he exclaimed a minute or two later. Graham was standing under a tree at the other side of the road, by the entrance to a lane. He had his head turned away from them, he was looking down the road.

'Pull in there.' Kelsey indicated an entry a few yards ahead. A van came along the road towards them, travelling towards Cannonbridge. As it approached Graham he stepped out from under the tree. The van was driven by a young man in dark greasy overalls. On the side of the vehicle was painted the name and address of a garage in a hamlet a quarter of a mile or so back from the road. The van halted barely long enough for Graham to jump in. The door slammed and the van went smartly off again.

Kelsey began to whistle, a single note, repeated in little bursts. After a minute or two he struck his knee. 'OK,' he said. 'The Parkfield estate. Take your time. Let the lad get in and settle down.'

Mrs Cooney came shuffling to the door in shapeless felt slippers. She looked at them warily, without surprise.

'If we could have a word with Graham,' Kelsey said.

'He's in the kitchen, having his supper.' She led the way along the passage. Through the open kitchen door they could see Graham sitting facing them across the table. He didn't look at them but kept his head lowered, he abandoned all attempt to eat. In front of him was a mug of tea and a plate with a half-eaten slice of bread and margarine, sprinkled with sugar. Mrs Cooney's cup stood next to the teapot, beside an open packet of sliced bread, a tub of margarine, a bag of sugar.

'No fish and chips, then?' Kelsey said to Graham on a jocular note as they entered the room. 'You've never gone and finished them already?' Graham made no reply but sat in the same frozen posture.

'You haven't come here to talk about fish and chips,' Mrs Cooney said. 'What do you want to ask him?' She dropped heavily into a chair, picked up her cup and took a long drink of tea.

Kelsey pulled back a chair and sat down. There was no fourth chair so Sergeant Lambert took up his stance leaning against the end of the dresser. Something white under the table caught his eye. He moved his head and saw that it was a crumpled handkerchief. He stooped and picked it up. He was about to hand it to Mrs Cooney when he saw that it wasn't a proper handkerchief but a square of old cotton sheeting, roughly torn, unhemmed. He hesitated, then put it down on the dresser. He glanced up and met Mrs Cooney's eye, aware, faintly amused.

'We just want a little chat with Graham,' Kelsey said.

'Then I wish you'd hurry up and be quick about it,' she retorted. 'I want him to finish his supper and get off to bed. He's tired, he hasn't been himself this last week or two. Must be the spring. Or growing pains.'

'Perhaps he's working too hard,' Kelsey suggested. She flashed him a sharp look but said nothing.

'Or maybe he's got something on his mind.'

'At his age?' Mrs Cooney said.

'How old are you?' Kelsey asked Graham.

He didn't look up. 'Twelve,' he answered in a low mumble.

'He'll be thirteen in October,' Mrs Cooney put in.

'I want you to take your mind back a few weeks,' Kelsey told Graham. 'To the evening of Wednesday, March 2nd.' Graham lowered his head even further and closed his eyes. 'The first Wednesday in March. Can you place that particular day in your mind?'

Graham gave a nod.

'Now, round about six or seven that evening, where were you? What were you doing?' Kelsey held up a hand. 'Before you say a word I'd better warn you not to waste our time with some cock-and-bull story about playing in the woods with your mates. We want the truth this time and we intend staying here till we get it.'

Graham made no response.

'A girl was murdered that evening,' Kelsey said. 'Brutally and horribly murdered. A girl only four or five years older than yourself, with the whole of her life before her. We have to catch the man who killed that girl—and her sister before her. A man who killed two girls in cold blood. And to do that we need to know what a great many people were doing that evening, we have to make it all slot together. If any of those people tells us lies, then it won't slot together properly and that man may go free.'

Graham remained mute and motionless. The silence lengthened. On the mantelshelf the alarm clock ticked loudly.

Mrs Cooney leaned suddenly forward. 'I don't know what it is you know,' she said to Graham with fierce urgency. 'But tell him, whatever it is. Tell him what he wants to know.'

Graham's head jerked up. He shot her an appalled, protesting look.

'Life and death,' she said in the same fierce tone. 'Nothing's more important than that. Tell him what he wants to know.'

'I can't.' Tears appeared in his eyes. 'He'll—'

'Never mind about that,' she said with finality. 'We've managed before, we'll manage again.'

He began to cry in earnest, he flung an arm across his face and sank down sobbing on the table.

'I'm making no bargain with you,' Kelsey told Mrs Cooney. 'I want that clearly understood. We've a pretty good idea where the boy was that evening, and what he was doing. We can't overlook it. You know as well as I do it's against the law for a lad under thirteen to take a job.'

'It's a relative,' Mrs Cooney protested. 'The man who owns the garage, he's a cousin of my husband. He thought he was doing us a good turn, letting Graham earn a few shillings.'

'Makes no difference who he is or what his intentions were. It's against the law.'

'But it's not as if it's heavy work,' she persisted. 'They look after him, see he doesn't strain himself. It's washing and polishing cars, mostly, fetching and carrying, brewing tea, running errands. Teaches him a bit about the trade, could be useful when he leaves school. Surely it's better than hanging about the streets, getting up to mischief, like most of the lads round here.'

'I don't deny any of that,' Kelsey said. 'But it's still against the law.'

She gave him a bleak look. 'It's all very well if you can afford to obey the law. We have to manage as best we can.'

'You'll be thirteen in October,' Kelsey said to Graham. 'It isn't all that long. You'll be able to go back to your job then.'

Graham raised his head and sat up. He dried his eyes on the sleeve of his jersey.

'You saw something that evening,' Kelsey said. 'What was it?'

'It was a car.' He looked directly at the Chief. He seemed calmer, more resigned. 'I was standing under the tree at the corner of the lane. I always stand there after I've got the fish and chips for Alan, he always has them for his supper.'

'Alan?'

'He's one of the mechanics at the garage.' Now that he had begun to talk, he answered readily. 'He lives near here, on the estate, he always gives me a lift home. I leave the garage before he does, so I can get the fish and chips while he's clearing up. I saw the car coming along the road—'

'In which direction?'

'It was coming from Cannonbridge. It signalled to turn right, to go down the lane by where I was standing.' Kelsey sat motionless. The lane led out to the field at Stoneleigh, passing within a mile or two of Fletcher's cottage. 'It had to wait,' Graham went on. 'There were some other cars coming along the road the other way. Then it turned and went past me, down the lane.' The room was very still; in the corner the ancient fridge coughed and sighed. 'The girl was in the front seat. She was laughing. She looked pleased and happy, a bit excited.' Mrs Cooney clasped her hands together.

'Did you recognize the girl?' Kelsey asked.

'I didn't recognize her then. But afterwards I knew who she was, from the posters, and her picture in the paper. It was Joanne Mowbray.' Kelsey lowered his head and sat with his eyes closed.

After a moment he said, 'It was more than a month after that evening when Joanne's picture appeared in the papers.

Can you be sure it was the same girl?'

'Yes, I'm quite sure,' Graham said with total certainty.

'Did you recognize the car?'

'Yes. He comes on the estate sometimes. If I'm here I look after his car for him, I make the other kids leave it alone. He gives me fifty pence.' He looked on the verge of tears again. Lambert saw a look of shocked incredulity cross Mrs Cooney's face. She put a hand up to her mouth.

'Whose car was it?' Kelsey asked.

'It was Mr Fletcher's.'

'You're certain it was Fletcher's car?'

'Yes. It's a green Range-Rover. I've often seen it.' He gave the registration number.

Kelsey's heart began to thump against his ribs. 'Did you see who was driving the car?'

Graham looked steadily back at him. 'Yes. It was Mr Fletcher.'

CHAPTER 16

There was a brief silence. Kelsey gave a long sigh.

'Only the other day,' Mrs Cooney exclaimed, still with an air of profound astonishment, 'Mr Fletcher said to me: Your lad's got a good head on his shoulders. Send him along to me when he leaves school. I can always use a bright, willing lad.' Graham began to draw sobbing breaths again but managed to control himself.

'Did either of them see you?' Kelsey asked him. 'Fletcher or the girl?'

'Mr Fletcher didn't see me. I'm not sure about the girl.' Tears trickled down his face, he dashed them fiercely aside. 'I think she saw me. She turned her head and looked my way, she was talking and laughing.'

'Can you describe her appearance?'

'She was wearing a green anorak with the hood back on her shoulders.'

'Anything else you remember?' Something solid and incontestable, Kelsey prayed, something that would stand up in court, that the lad couldn't have got from the newspapers, the posters, from gossip in the town; something the defence couldn't make mincemeat of inside two minutes.

Graham sat pondering. At last he said, 'She had a slide in her hair.' Kelsey could scarcely breathe. Graham put a hand up to the crown of his head. 'Her hair was bunched up on top, the slide held it up.'

'Can you describe the slide?'

'It was pretty big.' He gestured a size. 'It was green, with white markings, sort of mottled. It had a fancy shape, the top was curved.' His finger outlined a serpentine edge.

Kelsey sat back in his chair. That's it, he thought, that's one they can't shoot down. There had been no mention of the slide in press or radio handouts, in any of the published details.

'Afterwards,' he said, 'when you realized who it was you had seen that evening, why didn't you come forward and tell us?'

Graham stared down at the table. 'I didn't want to lose the job,' he said in a low voice. 'I knew if I told you, you'd find out I worked at the garage, and I'd have to stop.' He looked up at the Chief. 'We need the money.'

'Did you mention what you'd seen to anyone else?'

'I didn't say anything about it later on, when I knew who the girl was, but I told Alan at the time that I'd just seen Mr Fletcher's Range-Rover go down the lane. I said it was the sort of car I'd like to have one day if I was rich. Alan said he'd rather have a Jaguar. We had a bit of an argument about cars, which were the best.'

'Did you mention to Alan that you'd seen a girl in the car with Mr Fletcher?'

'Yes, I did. Alan was laughing and joking about the

Jaguar. He said girls always go for a car like that, they wouldn't look at a Range-Rover if there was a Jaguar about. I said Mr Fletcher had a girl with him in the Range-Rover. He asked me what she was like, if she was pretty. I said she was all right.'

'Suppose I said to you that perhaps it wasn't that Wednesday evening that you saw the Range-Rover with Fletcher and the girl inside, maybe it was the Monday or Tuesday of that week?' The defence would try to tie the lad up in knots.

'No, it was definitely that Wednesday,' Graham answered without hesitation. 'When I read about it in the papers I thought about it a lot, and I'm quite sure it was that Wednesday, the second of March.'

'How can you be so sure?'

'Because of two things. One was that Mr Fletcher had been on the estate a few days before, on the Saturday. He came with some people from the council. They had a photographer and a reporter with them, from the *Journal*.'

'That's right,' Mrs Cooney put in. 'They were taking pictures of what it's like round here before they start the improvments. They talked to a lot of people on the estate, I was talking to them myself. There were some photos in the paper on the Thursday.'

'That would be Thursday, March 3rd?' Kelsey said.

'I can soon tell you the date. I kept the paper because of the photos.' She went over to a cupboard. 'I'm in one of the photos and Graham's in another. Yes, here it is, March 3rd.' She opened up the paper as she came back to the table. 'There you are.' She set it down in front of the Chief: a double spread about the proposed improvements at Parkfield. Half a dozen photographs, one showing a group of four men, among them Fletcher, talking to a knot of householders, one of them Mrs Cooney. On the opposite page a photograph of a particularly dilapidated dwelling, with a Range-Rover drawn up nearby, Graham Cooney standing guard over it.

'I mentioned that to Alan,' Graham said, 'when I told him

I'd just seen Mr Fletcher drive down the lane. I said Mr Fletcher had been on the estate the Saturday before, he'd given me fifty pence for looking after the Range-Rover. Alan made a joke about it.'

'And the other thing?' Kelsey said. 'The other reason you were so sure it was on the Wednesday that you saw Fletcher?'

'It was because of the film. They were showing a James Bond film on television that evening. It was *Casino Royal*. Alan likes James Bond films, he always watches them when they're on TV. *Casino Royal*'s one of his favourites, he was in a hurry to get home to watch it. When we were saying about the sort of cars we'd like to have, Alan started talking about the cars in the Bond films, and about James Bond's girls— because of the film being on that evening.'

'I expect you and Alan often talk about cars and girls when he gives you a lift home.'

'No, we don't usually talk about anything, we're both usually tired. Alan isn't much of a talker anyway. It was just that evening, with me seeing Mr Fletcher drive down the lane, that started it.'

'What time was it when you saw the Range-Rover? Try to be as exact as possible.'

'We don't finish at the same time every evening, it depends how busy we are. They usually lock up around six or half past, maybe a quarter to seven. I always leave before Alan, to get the fish and chips while he's clearing up. That day Alan told me he didn't want to be late, because of the film. I was to be sure to go for the fish and chips by a quarter past six at the latest. And I did, I ran all the way, I was standing waiting for him by the tree quite a few minutes before he came along. When he picked me up he said: Jump in, it's ten to and the film starts at seven. It was a few minutes before that when I saw the Range-Rover, that would make it about a quarter to seven.'

'Afterwards, when you read about the murders, did you talk to Alan about what you'd seen that evening?' Graham shook his head. 'Did you ever speak to Alan again about having seen the Range-Rover that evening?' Again he shook his head. 'Why not?' Kelsey asked.

'I thought he'd make me go to the police, and if I wouldn't go, then he'd go himself, and I'd lose my job.' He drew a little sobbing breath. 'After a bit I tried to forget about it.'

'We'll have Alan's address,' Kelsey said. When Graham had given him the details Kelsey pushed back his chair and stood up. 'Is there some neighbour you can get to come and sit with the children?' he asked Mrs Cooney. 'We'll have to take a statement from Graham and that's best done down at the station. We'd like you to be there with him.'

When they came into the station some time later, Constable Jago was sitting in the reception area, reading the evening paper; he had been sitting there well over an hour. He glanced up as they came in. He sprang to his feet and went rapidly over to the Chief. Kelsey looked at him with sharp inquiry.

'I found the shop that sold the bracelet,' Jago told him. 'I'm afraid I didn't get the name of the man who bought it.' He retailed his conversation, the shopkeeper's recollection of the incident, of the customer who had beaten him down. 'But he was sure he'd be able to recognize him again,' he added. 'He said he was tall and well built, well dressed and well groomed, with well-kept hands—but the tip of one of his fingers, the middle finger of the left hand, was missing.'

It was a bright, cold, blowy night. Kelsey and Lambert sat in the car park at the Memorial Hall. Fletcher's green Range-Rover was parked a few yards away from them. From time to time a burst of applause inside the hall signalled the end of one speech or the beginning of another. Sergeant Lambert had fallen into a somnolent, dreamlike state that was not unpleasant. Kelsey's fierce restlessness and brief bout of euphoria had both drained away. All he felt now was a bone-deep fatigue, a powerful longing to be done with the rest of the night, drive off home, get his head down for a long, long sleep.

A minute or two after half past ten there came a sustained burst of applause, followed by the sound of concerted movement. The doors of the hall were thrust open and fastened back. The audience surged out, arguing, discussing. Not a night to stand about in; they buttoned up their coats and hurried to their cars with heads bent against the pouncing wind.

The crowd thinned, the cars moved off, the exodus dwindled to a straggle, finally died away. Kelsey got out of the car and Lambert followed him across to the hall. Kelsey halted by a window; through a gap in the curtains he could see two or three middle-aged women moving briskly about, tidying up. At the end of the hall an older woman with blue-rinsed hair was talking earnestly to someone outside the Chief's field of vision.

Kelsey shifted his position and saw that it was Fletcher. He wore a dark business suit and a white shirt; he carried a coat over one arm. He stood listening to the blue-rinsed woman with close attention; he looked lively and stimulated, pleased with his evening. Then he glanced at his watch, smiled and said something to the woman. He called out a good night to the other helpers, he turned towards the exit. The woman began to gather up leaflets abandoned on the seats of chairs.

The two policemen walked round to the open doorway and stood to one side, screened by the angle of the door.

Fletcher came into the vestibule. He glanced out at the light-spattered evening, up at the sky. He began to put on his coat. He exuded an air of enormous confidence, unflagging energy.

Kelsey moved into view. Fletcher stood frozen for an instant, his coat half way on to his shoulders, then he recovered himself.

'Chief Inspector!' he said on an easy, rallying note. 'I'm afraid you're too late for the meeting. You must come along to the next one.' He shrugged on his coat, adjusted the set about his shoulders.

'I must ask you to accompany us to the station,' Kelsey said in a formal tone. 'There are some questions we'd like to ask you.'

'At this time of night?' Fletcher said in a voice of friendly protest. 'I've had a very long day. Surely tomorrow will do.'

'We have a witness,' Kelsey told him. 'A cast-iron witness who saw you driving Joanne Mowbray in the direction of Stoneleigh on the evening of Wednesday, March 2nd.'

Fletcher stood gazing out at them in silence.

'I must ask you,' Kelsey said again, 'to accompany us to the station.'

The inner door opened and the blue-rinsed woman put her head into the vestibule. 'Mr Fletcher,' she called. 'Glad I've caught you. The coffee morning on Thursday—will you be able to look in?'

He turned his head and looked back at her, half-smiling. 'I don't know that I should bank on it,' he told her, his voice light and clear. She said good night again and went back inside.

Fletcher buttoned his coat with a sudden access of energy. He came down the steps and they fell into position on either side of him. They walked without speaking past the posters with Fletcher's face looking out, smiling and resolute, radiating energy and purpose.

Round the corner of the building the wind lay in wait for them. Fletcher turned up his collar against the chill blast. Over the night air came the distant rumble and clatter of a train. They walked across the car park in silence, under a vast, cold, arching sky, glittering with stars.